A GAME OF KILL

ROCKFORD SECURITY MYSTERY SERIES

L. A. DOBBS

1

―――――

*D**eath is never pretty.*

Mike McQuade stared into the bright turquoise waters of the El Cortez swimming pool and would have chuckled, would have shaken his head ruefully and shrugged his shoulders at the absurdity of his situation. Would have, except for the body in front of him—a single, jagged stab wound straight through the heart. The air around him smelled of copper and chlorine and condemnation.

Using his foot, he carefully rolled her over onto her back. The tiled floor around her was wet, but she was bone dry. He was careful not to disturb any of the fine details that had been staged so precisely or the blood pooled around her chest. He already knew what he'd see, already knew exactly the face that would stare back at him, already regretted his decision, his actions.

Still, when her face came into view, her kohl-rimmed, glassy blue eyes locked on him—forever shocked, forever damning. They reminded him of another set of eyes, just as dazed and accusing, just as familiar, just as dead. That one had been his fault too. Another check for his should-have-seen-it-coming column. Another mark against him.

A sound echoed from somewhere in the distance and Mike glanced up quick before refocusing his attention back to the woman. He didn't have much time. Someone would discover this gruesome scene soon enough, and he wanted to make sure he was long gone by then. But first he wanted to retain as much detail about her as possible. It would help him later.

My redemption rests in those details.

She was dressed in 1940s finery, her dark hair had been meticulously wound into Victory rolls, and her lips were painted bright red. The woman looked like she belonged on a Vargas calendar or a Hollywood noir film set. Her outfit had been planned down to the last detail —crimson polka-dot calf-length cocktail dress with a sweetheart neckline to accentuate her curves, fishnet hose with the seams up the back and black, high-heeled Mary Janes. Even the black feather barrette decorating her elaborate coiffure was all done to perfection and all designed to send a message.

A message Mike had seen before.

After all, he'd created it.

He glanced at the cryptic text still highlighting the screen of his disposable cell phone, the words a jumble of 1940s slang—*Dumb Dora Framed a Fall. Oops. She's All Wet Now*—then back to the corpse once more. Even distorted by death, her pretty face still had him recalling happier times, times before he'd become the privacy-hoarding hermit he was today.

Voices echoed down the quiet hall leading toward the pool, and Mike knew his quiet interlude had ended. Wouldn't be long now until this place swarmed with cops and investigators and the press.

God, the press.

Always hounding him, always chasing him. Never satisfied, never truthful.

After one final nod to the woman sprawled poolside, Mike pushed to his feet and hurried over to a trash can along the far wall near the exit, his shoulders hunched and his hands shoved deep into the pockets of his hoodie. His hard-won privacy was far too precious to risk it all now, no matter how tempting.

Nothing more I can do here.

He repeated the phrase over and over in his head, like maybe if he said it enough he'd actually believe it someday. Not now. Not really. But someday. If he was lucky.

Once he performed a factory reset on the phone to erase his information, Mike wiped it down to remove any traceable fingerprints. All those crazy fans and hackers who stalked him day and night would have a field day if they saw him now. One more reason he used disposable phones. New number, new identity, new chance to escape the ghosts that haunted him. At least for those few brief days before it was time to switch again.

Before tossing the device into the trash, he performed one last service for the woman. One last noble act in a string of actions that had been anything but chivalrous. He dialed 9-1-1 then dumped the phone in the garbage and slipped out the shadowed side exit just as two female hotel employees walked in.

Their horrified screams chased him into the darkness outside.

2

———

Laura Rockford leaned sideways to peer past the traffic backed up down Sixth Street. Of course, on the one day she treated herself to a coffee on the way to see her big brother there would be an accident holding everything up. Blake was such a stickler about promptness, he'd never let her tardiness slide. She exhaled and flopped back into the driver's seat of her five-year-old Impala. Seemed she was always running one step behind these days—in work and in life.

The guy behind her honked, and without thinking Laura leaned out the window and flashed him the bird. Her siblings were always telling her she was too rash, too get-up-in-someone's-grill. Still, it was a skill that served her well as a reporter, and she didn't have any intention of changing her personality any time soon.

She took a long sip of her coffee and watched as two

squad cars, sirens wailing and lights blazing, swerved around the corner about half a block ahead and parked on the sidewalk outside the historic El Cortez Hotel.

Finally, something interesting.

Instincts on high alert, Laura nosed her car out of the line of traffic and into a parking spot along the curb then grabbed her messenger bag and coffee and popped open the door. She'd been on the hunt for the next big story, the one that might finally break her into the big time, since she'd taken the staff reporter job at the *Las Vegas Chronicle* newspaper. It was the area's most widely read and prestigious paper, but with her straight out of journalism school and with few bylines to her name, her editor stuck Laura with all the fluff—pieces on casino openings and local celebrities having babies or buying houses.

She wanted real stories, real hard-hitting news.

A chance to prove I'm more than my family thinks I can be.

More than I think I can be.

She checked her appearance in her rearview mirror —same hazel eyes, same wavy, wild brown hair, same old ordinary face staring back—then smoothed a hand down her jeans-covered thighs and got out of the car. In her plain white T-shirt and sneakers, she looked just like another tourist, exactly what she needed to blend in, to go unseen.

Determined, she pushed through the gawkers

surrounding the crime scene and ducked under the yellow tape while the officer in charge of crowd control was otherwise occupied with a group of tourists angling for selfies. It had rained sometime the night before, and the warm desert air was unusually humid. Puddles dotted the pavement, and the smell of damp permeated the air around her. She made it as far as windows overlooking the indoor pool before she spied two uniformed officers heading her way. *Crap.* With only a few seconds to make this visit count, Laura pulled out her cell phone to videotape the scene inside—a body lying poolside, a woman wearing what appeared to be vintage clothing. Blood pooled near her chest, and one of her hands was outstretched toward Laura as if begging her to solve the mystery.

"Excuse me, ma'am," one of the approaching officers said. "The public's not allowed to be in here."

"I'm not the public." Laura eased her phone back into her pocket before the officers thought to confiscate it. "I'm a reporter for the *Chronicle*. Is Detective Atkins here?"

"No, he isn't. And even if he was, he warned us about you," the second officer said.

"Me?" Laura placed an insincere hand over her chest.

"Yeah, you. You're Blake Rockford's little sister. And even worse, the press." Each officer took an arm, and together they escorted her back toward the taped-off perimeter. Officer number two held up the tape and gestured with his hand for her to sidle underneath it. "Come back here again, Miss Rockford, we'll arrest you for trespassing. Detective Atkins's orders."

"What about my First Amendment rights?" She squared her shoulders and met their gazes directly. She'd been raised with alpha men galore and never backed down from a fight. It took a hell of a lot more than some puffed-up male bravado to scare her off.

"What about 'em?" Officer number one snickered then walked away with his partner. "Have a nice day."

"Can you tell me anything about the victim?" she yelled after them. "The crime scene? Anything?"

They just kept on walking, with not even a glance back in her direction.

Dammit. Laura weaved her way through the crowd back to her Impala. At least she'd managed to get some footage of the scene. Maybe there might be a lead in there somewhere. She'd ask Blake about it when...

Oh, crap.

A glance at her watch showed she was now almost forty-five minutes late for her meeting. Blake would have a cow, if he hadn't shit an entire herd already.

At least the traffic jam had cleared by the time she headed the few blocks north to the Rockford Security offices. Five minutes later, she walked into the lobby and waved to the receptionist with one hand, her coffee clutched in the other, as she headed toward her oldest brother's digs. As CEO of the family business, he had the largest office in the place—stark and modern, everything contemporary and cool and just a smidge intimidating. Not unlike the man himself. According to her friends, he looked like a swoon-worthy quarterback, with his dark hair and steely eyes, but to her he was just Big Bro.

Blake wasn't in his office when she arrived, so Laura went in anyway and made herself at home, pulling out her phone to check the footage she'd shot at the El Cortez. With any luck, there might be something usable. Except there wasn't. Her degree from the University of Las Vegas was in journalism, not cinematography, obviously. Every panoramic shot of the poolside scene shook and was out of focus. Good thing she excelled at the written word, because she sucked at the visual side of things.

"About time you showed up," Blake said, coming up behind her. He closed the door behind him, then leaned down to kiss her on the cheek. "Some of us do have schedules to keep."

"I have schedules, too. Mine are just more flexible. One of the perks of the job."

He raised a disparaging brow at her, giving her his infamous glare. The Hurt, everyone had nicknamed it. She wasn't ruffled. Blake might talk a good game, might look one too, but underneath his tough-guy exterior, her big brother was nothing but a marshmallow.

He sighed and squinted over her shoulder. "What are you watching? Looks like a ticket to seasickness."

"Funny." She glanced sideways at him. "I stopped by a crime scene on my way here. That's why I was late. Over at the El Cortez. Appears a female was murdered near their pool. I can't figure out why she's dressed in vintage clothing, though."

"I can." Blake straightened and walked around to take a seat behind his desk. "It's a game."

"Game, huh? What kind of game?" Laura clicked off the phone and stared at him. "Sickos R Us?"

"No. A video game. Local guy designed it and made a killing. No pun intended." He grinned. "It's called *Vegas Noir*, I think. First game his company made. Tech empire called M Cubed, office downtown."

"Never heard of it."

"Anyway, I met the guy a couple of years ago, at the release party for *Vegas Noir*. I was still a detective on the force at the time. He seemed nice enough, in that weird geeky gamer sort of way."

"Huh." She slid her phone back into her trusty messenger bag—the thing never left her side—and instead pulled out the notebook and pen she always carried in the side pocket for quick access. After flipping to a new blank page, she started taking notes. "So this guy lives here in town? This game creator?"

"Yeah." Blake sat forward, his expression shifting from indulgent to annoyed. "But that's not why you made this appointment with me today, Sis. Why are you here? Not that I don't like seeing you more often than the family dinners."

She glanced over at the large ficus in the corner, her present to her brother upon his grand opening and the only color in the otherwise neutral room. "Bertha's still going strong."

"She's a staple around here, an inaugural member of the team. Can't have Rockford Security without Bertha." He sat back again and clasped his hands over his lean stomach. "Now tell me the truth. No more bullshit or evading. You are here. Why?"

Laura sighed. No matter how old she got, Blake still had that ability to make her feel five again. "I came to see if you might have any interesting leads about some of your cases." She twiddled the notebook in her fingers. "Now, I guess fate just dropped this into my lap, and, unless my journalistic instincts are way off, this is gonna be a murder worth a front-page story." She gave him a coy smile and a wink. Of course, this might turn out to be nothing, but she couldn't shake the feeling that there was more to this story than a simple drowning. Both her interest and her instincts were piqued, which was rare.

"How do you know what happened at the El Cortez was a murder?" Blake narrowed his gaze at her, his index fingers tapping against his bottom lip. He reminded her of one of her favorite stodgy old professors back in college. The guy had covered World War II and Vietnam and ate undergrads for breakfast. Everyone except for Laura.

"Who dresses up like a 1940s pin-up gal to end themselves?" So obviously not a suicide. "What's this guy's name? The one you met at the party who owns this tech company."

"Mike McQuade. Why?"

"Bet he'd love knowing someone's using his games to stage murders."

"No one wants to know that." Blake frowned. "Please tell me you won't stalk this poor man. And for heaven's sake, stay out of his penthouse."

"No promises. He's a public figure, by virtue of his business. If someone's using his games for nefarious purposes, then the world deserves to know."

Blake snorted. "Nefarious purposes? Break out the thesaurus much?"

Laura stuck her tongue out at him and continued to write. "What's Mike McQuade look like?" Blake opened his mouth to answer, but she held up a hand to stop him, a mental picture developing. "Wait. You said weird, geeky gamer. I'm imagining Coke-bottle glasses and high-water pants. Maybe a pocket protector thrown in for good measure?"

"Nah. The guy was nice and normal looking, I guess." He wrinkled his nose. "I don't spend a lot of time considering other guys' appearances, unless they're suspects."

"Give me a general vibe. From what you remember."

"Promise me you will not hound this guy, Sis."

"I'll only do what's necessary to get to the truth, how about that?"

He gave her an incredulous look then sighed. "Fine. A couple inches shorter than me, dark hair, lean build. That's all I know."

"And he lives where, did you say?"

"I didn't." Blake smiled, all even white teeth and tight-lipped confidence. "Nice try, though."

"Thanks." Laura tossed her long, russet-colored hair over her shoulder, basking in her brother's praise. "Do you know where I can find this Mr. McQuade? Just to ask him a few innocent questions."

"I doubt you've ever made the acquaintance of an innocent question."

She grinned. "C'mon, Blake. Give a girl a bone here. Where does he live? If he's into technology, he's probably doing pretty well. Queensridge? Seven Hills, maybe?"

"Nah." Blake squeezed the bridge of his nose between his thumb and forefinger. "If my memory serves me correctly, the party was at his residence. The penthouse suite of those fancy condos at the north end of the Strip."

"Turnberry Place?"

"Yeah. That's it."

"Great." Laura flipped her notebook closed and stood. "Well, I guess I'm off, then."

"Hey." Blake pushed to his feet as well and came

around the desk to join her. "You want to grab some lunch or something? Dino and I were supposed to go, but something came up with Jan's tour schedule and he can't make it."

"Oh, I'm sorry, Big Bro." She stood on tiptoe to kiss his cheek. "Maybe some other time."

Laura took off toward the door then smiled at him over her shoulder. "Today, I've got some snooping to do."

AN HOUR LATER, after another stop at the 1020 Café for fresh brew and bribes, Laura headed into police headquarters. The gals stationed behind the reception desk in the large, brightly lit lobby knew her and waved her inside.

She spotted her quarry near the back of the room, his attention diverted by his computer screen. Perfect. Laura made her way through the crowded precinct room toward the cubicle of one Detective Troy Atkins, Homicide Division.

"Howdy." She plunked a fresh double espresso and a big, fat brownie down in front of him. "Long time no see."

"Well, if it isn't my favorite nosy reporter." Troy swiveled his chair to face her and grinned. Most women she knew went wild for his cover-model good looks—tawny, sun-streaked brown hair, chiseled jaw, green-gold eyes that seemed to glow when he smiled. Good thing Laura wasn't most women, or she'd melt into a puddle of goo at the sexy little grin he was giving her now. "What can I do for you, Laura?"

The low, rough tone of his voice, along with the spark of heat in his eyes, suggested there was more to his question than work. He'd been after her to go out with him for two years. So far, she hadn't relented. Not that she hadn't been tempted. Even a workaholic like her made time for fine man-candy like him, but the timing had never been right to develop their flirtation into something more. Still wasn't. Laura avoided his eager-puppy gaze and took a seat in one of the two chairs in front of his desk, setting her messenger bag on the other. "Can't a girl just stop by to say hello and bring her favorite cop a treat?"

"Sure." He popped the lid off his cup and inhaled the steam rising from it like a junkie taking a hit of meth. Like any reporter worth her salt, Laura was well aware of his weaknesses—strong black coffee, beautiful women, sugar—and she wasn't above using them against him when necessary. Too bad he knew her buttons to push as well. "But that's not why you're here, is it?"

"Why does everyone question my motives today?"

He raised a brow at her, sipping his coffee, staring at her over the rim.

"Fine. I need a name. That's all. Just one name..."

"Ah, a name." He nodded, his smile cryptic. "And whose name might you be needing?"

"There was an incident this morning over on Sixth and Fremont, at the El Cortez. I happened to be driving by, so I stopped to check it out and—"

"Trespassed on a crime scene. Yes, I know."

Laura frowned. "I did not trespass."

"Really? My beat cops told a different story. Pardon me if I take their word over yours." He grinned. "I hope you didn't compromise evidence."

"I would never."

"Laura, Laura, Laura." He leaned forward to rest his muscular forearms on the desk. "When will you learn that I have eyes and ears everywhere?"

"Fine." She sat back and crossed her arms. "I might've done a bit of creative wandering while I was there, but it was all in the name of journalism, and I never compromised anything. I didn't even get within ten feet of that body. That's why I'm here, actually. I'm hoping you can tell me the name of the victim."

"I can't, Laura." He sighed, his smile fading. "You know that. Against regulations."

She scrunched her nose. She hadn't wanted to play her trump card, but she really needed that name. "I'll keep it private, I promise. Consider it a personal favor, just between you and me."

"A favor, huh?" He seemed to consider her offer, his

warm gaze narrowing. "Still haven't collected on all those other 'favors' yet."

"I can't help it if I'm busy, Troy."

"A beautiful woman like you shouldn't work so hard." He reached across the desk to trace his finger over the back of her hand. "Have dinner with me later this week?"

Laura's stomach knotted. It wasn't that she didn't like Troy. He was nice enough, in a muscled-god, baby-faced-boy kind of way, but once she got hooked on a story, she was like a horse with blinders. All she saw, all she ate, slept, and drank was that story. And right now, the body at the El Cortez was her new story. Still, she had to keep him interested long enough to give her what she needed. Besides, one dinner couldn't hurt anything. "Maybe. You give me the name and I'll check my calendar."

He cursed and turned away from her to face his computer. "Look, even if I wanted to tell you, I couldn't. The victim had no ID, and so far there's been no matches on fingerprints or dental records. Once we do get the match, the detectives have to notify the next of kin before we can release that information. You know the procedure, Laura. Hell, your brother followed it for years. What if the victim's family happened to see something in the paper about their loved one before they'd been notified by the department? Think how they'd feel. Think of the liability this department would face. There'd be hell to pay, and rightly so. Understand?"

"Understood." She slumped in her seat and stared at the mounds of paperwork on his desk while he typed on his keyboard, his back to her. At the top of one messy pile were several snapshots—a red polka-dot dress, a fishnet-covered foot, dark hair styled in an elaborate 1940s-style hairdo.

The crime scene.

Pulse pounding, Laura leaned forward again, slowly, so as not to draw Troy's attention.

If I can just get a peek at those...

"So, I suppose that means dinner's off?" Troy asked, his gaze still focused on his computer screen. "You know we really should give this thing between us a try. We have a lot in common. We're both Las Vegas natives, both raised in big families, both too smart for our own good."

With her breath held, Laura gently nudged a stack of papers out of the way to see the scrawled notes beneath it on the corner of one photo—disposable cell phone found in trash. Sent to IT for analysis. Need to question McQuade.

Huh. Why would they need to question Mike McQuade about the victim's cell phone? And why couldn't they ID her from the SIM card inside? Most importantly, how involved was Mike McQuade in all of this? I'm apparently not the only one investigating his link to the murder this morning. His game, his scene, his kill?

Laura shook her head to clear it. She'd been trained to connect the dots between disparate facts and draw conclusions, but the jump from some whacko using imagery from McQuade's video game as inspiration for the murder to Mike McQuade committing said murder himself was far too big, especially at this early stage.

Still, the cops must suspect he'd had some involvement if they wanted to question him.

That settled it.

She needed to talk to him, the sooner the better.

At her lack of response, Troy turned to face her again and took her hand before she could pull away. "Listen, Laura, I know why you come in here and this whole cat-and-mouse game we play is all in good fun, but I'd really like to have dinner with you. Get to know you better." He gestured toward the rest of the room with his free hand. "Outside of all this craziness. What do you say?"

"I—" Laura pushed to her feet and yanked free. "I think that sounds nice, Troy. How about I call you later and we can set something up?"

"Yeah." His flat tone suggested he didn't believe her at all. "Whatever."

"Okay, then. Talk to you soon." She hustled out of there like her butt was on fire. It wasn't that she didn't like Troy or wasn't attracted to him. He was fine. She just didn't have time to deal with a relationship right now. Not with him. Not with anyone. She had goals and dreams and a budding career, and getting involved in a serious relationship would only jeopardize those aspirations.

Disappointed, she waved to the gals at the reception

desk on her way out. She'd really hoped to get more information about the victim, but all she'd ended up with was another runaround. Either Troy really didn't have the information, or he'd been lying.

Either way, all she had now was a vague description of some tech head whose game may or may not be involved with this whole sordid deal. And a vague address. As she climbed in behind the wheel of her white sedan, she cringed. Going into a story blind wasn't ideal, but it didn't look like she had much choice in the matter. She eased her car out of its parking spot and headed back toward her apartment downtown.

She was on to something here. She could feel it in her bones.

Now she just had to find a clue, any clue, to lead her in the right direction.

3

———

Laura walked into her apartment and was struck by a pang of guilt.

Not because her sister Olivia stood waiting for her at the counter because she was running late again. She glanced around at her messy place. No. She felt guilty because she should've tried to clean up before her guest arrived. At least she thought that's what normal people did. People who weren't busy pursuing their life goals, anyway.

Liv, of course, was doing what Liv always did best—looking perfect, acting perfect, being perfect. Perfect long, dark hair. Perfect cat-like green eyes. Perfect body in her perfect clothes. Growing up, Laura had often felt overshadowed by her older sister's dazzling lack of imperfections. Now... now it just was what it was. Liv was perfect and Laura... wasn't.

Oh, well.

She tossed her messenger bag on a table beside the door and walked into the kitchen. "What's up?"

Her sister gave her a small smile and pointed at a foil-covered pan on the counter. "Brought you a casserole from Mom." She leaned back against the breakfast bar on her elbows while Laura pulled a bottle of water from her fridge. She offered Liv one too, but she declined. "Good thing I had it with me, since there's nothing else to eat around here. Not to mention the fact lunch was an hour ago."

"I planned to go to the grocery store later." Laura cracked open her water and took a sip. "And I'm sorry. I got caught in a meeting at the police station."

"Arrested again, huh?"

"Funny. No. I was trying to dig up some information for a new story."

"You invited me to lunch today."

"We can still go out, if you want. An early dinner."

Liv shook her head. "Even the early-bird specials don't start until four. Admit it. You forgot about me."

"I did not. I just got wrapped up in other things and lost track of time."

"You could've texted me."

"My battery died," Laura said, her tone sheepish. "Look, I'm sorry, okay? You know how I get when I'm working."

"Yeah, I do. Because I'm the same way." Olivia

grinned. "Must be the Rockford gene."

"Must be." Laura took another gulp of water then screwed the lid back on, feeling a bit underdressed compared to her sister's designer pantsuit chic. But the nature of Laura's work demanded a more casual vibe, professional yet functional, able to accommodate a variety of situations at a moment's notice. Liv's attire was a reflection of her status—sleek, black, tailor-made trousers and jacket paired with a crisp white shirt. The whole ensemble practically screamed corporate power bitch. As COO of Rockford Security, Liv was used to proving herself in a man's world, and it showed in her austere dress and brusque manner.

Yet underneath all that business armor resided the sister she loved. The sister who'd taught her all the self-defense moves she knew. The sister who loved gossip as much as Laura did, even if she'd never admit it.

"So." Liv tossed her long chocolate-brown hair over her shoulder and faced Laura. "Heard you stopped by the office this morning and didn't bother to say hi to your big sis." She placed a dramatic hand over her heart and winced. "I'm hurt."

"Like I said, I'm working on something." She went through the stack of days-old mail on her side table. Bills she set to one side, the rest got tossed into the trash, unopened.

"Tell me about it."

"What? My new story?"

"Yeah." Liv started tidying some of the clutter in the living room, neatly stacking the scattered newspapers and folding several scarves Laura had tossed over the back of the sofa on her way in or out of the place. "Anything interesting?"

"Not sure yet. On my way to see Blake, I came across a crime scene. Woman. Looked to be in her mid-thirties. Killed near the pool at the El Cortez. When I showed the footage on my phone to Blake, he immediately thought of some video game he'd seen a year or so ago. He mentioned knowing the developer. Local guy named Mike McQuade. I went to the police station to see if I could get any more info on the victim."

"*The* Mike McQuade?"

"Yeah. Why?" She joined Liv in the living room and shoved aside several half-read magazines and a couple of balled-up sweaters so they could both sit down. "You know him too?"

"No." Liv winked. "All I know is what I've seen in the local society columns. He's the hot new bachelor in town. And not just for his technical skills."

"Oh." At this point, Laura didn't care what he looked like. All she wanted to know was if he'd had something to do with that woman's death this morning. "Well, it seems he might be in trouble."

"Really?" Liv leaned in closer. "Why? Did he have something to do with the murder? What did you find out?"

"Nothing concrete yet, but from what Blake told me about his game and what I saw this morning, there might be a connection between him and the victim."

"You're kidding."

"Nope. What else can you tell me about him?"

"Not much. Like I said, I've never met him personally. From what I've read, though, he's pretty reclusive. Keeps to himself, doesn't go out much, very mysterious."

"Huh." Laura shrugged. "Well, I guess I can find out more later at his place."

Liv straightened. "Tell me you're not thinking of going over there. How do you even know where he lives?"

"Blake mentioned it earlier today. And yeah. I need to talk to him to find out what he knows. This could be my big break, Sis. My shot at a national spot. I can't let it slip away."

"I'm not sure going over there is a good idea, Laura. What if this guy *is* involved in that woman's death somehow? You can't just walk into a killer's home and accuse him of murder."

"I'm not an idiot." Laura crossed her arms. She appreciated her sister's concern, but nothing worth pursuing came risk free. Besides, the guy sat behind a computer all day. How dangerous could he be? "I just want to talk to the guy. Butter him up a little. See if I can find out more about him. And what entrepreneur doesn't like talking about their business, right? Don't worry. I can take care of myself. I learned from the best, remember?"

"Yeah." Liv gave her a self-satisfied grin. "You were my best student."

"Yep." Laura fist-pumped the air. "Girls rule."

"Damn straight." Liv's stomach growled, and she chuckled. "Mind if I heat up some of Mom's casserole?"

"Nah, help yourself. I'll never eat all of that anyway. What did she send this time?"

Laura followed her sister back into the kitchen and said a silent prayer of thanks that she'd at least remembered to run the dishwasher the other night. Accepting food donations from her family was one thing. Having them pity her for her complete lack of housekeeping skills was another. It wasn't that she liked living in a post-party dorm-room environment. She just had better things to do with her time. Like work.

Liv fixed them each a plate of homemade mac and cheese, and they resettled on the sofa to eat. It was the first hot, home-cooked meal Laura had had since the last Rockford get-together a month prior, and the delicious food and the love put into making it were the equivalent of a warm security blanket.

"Tell me more about what this guy looks like," Laura said around a bite of cheesy goodness as she booted up her laptop. A quick Google search brought up the website for McQuade's company, M Cubed, as well as several buy links for his games. No pictures of him on the site, though. She didn't have much time to sit around and play video games, but this was all in the name of research. Laura set her plate aside and got up to dig her wallet out of her messenger bag.

"What are you doing?" Liv asked around a mouthful of pasta.

"I'm going to download his game, *Vegas Noir*, to see what it's like. If it's got something to do with these murders, then it might give me some leads." She returned to the couch and typed in her credit card info then pushed Purchase. Minutes later the game opened on her screen.

Liv leaned in closer to peer at her screen. "That looks pretty cool. Very old Vegas, Rat Pack style."

"Yeah." Laura quickly zipped through the instructions then chose her character, a James Cagney–style gangster. "You want to play too?" She glanced at her sister.

"Sure." Liv shrugged and reached over to tap a few keys on the laptop. "There. Now I'm Veronica Lake."

"Nice."

Together they explored the virtual world Mike had created. Everything was quite detailed, from the setting to the clothing to the dialogue. They made it through half of the first level before they were both out of XP points and their characters were dead in the street in front of the old Glitter Gulch Casino.

"Well, that was interesting." Liv snorted and set her

empty dish aside.

"Yeah." Laura rolled her stiff neck and closed the laptop. Almost an hour had passed in what seemed like seconds. No wonder people called those games such time sucks. She never lost track of time that way. "I still need to get a better idea of what this Mike McQuade looks like before I head to his place. Don't want to pass him in the hall without knowing it."

"Here." Liv grabbed her phone from her pocket. "I can show you."

"Really?" Laura watched Liv thumb McQuade's name into her browser. Seconds later a bevy of results came up, including several pictures. She passed the phone to Laura and smiled. "Pretty hot, right?"

"Yeah, he's okay I guess." Tall and lean, with brown hair and eyes, his scruffy stubble, Buddy Holly glasses, and casual-chic designer hoodie and jeans pegged him as a typical hipster. Definitely not the uber-nerd she'd expected. "If you go for that whole dark and mysterious type."

Which she did.

Her sister's expression hovered somewhere between polite disinterest and "I told you so."

She scrolled to the next shot of Mike. This time he was facing the camera, a shadow of darkness lurking behind his chocolate gaze. Dressed this time in a tailored black suit, his shoulders were slightly hunched, as if deflecting a hard blow. She couldn't help but wonder who or what had hurt him, couldn't help wanting to defend him. The text below the picture mentioned him leaving the funeral of a close friend.

Sympathy joined the curiosity bubbling inside her.

She handed the phone back to her sister fast. Nope. Not going there. Her integrity as a journalist required her to remain impartial. If she wanted this story to work, she could not develop feelings for this Mike McQuade, no matter how innocent.

"Seen enough, huh?" Liv took the phone back, the look in her green eyes far too perceptive for Laura's liking. "He's cute. But that doesn't mean you shouldn't be cautious. Ted Bundy was cute, too."

"I'm always cautious." Laura pushed to her feet and took their empty plates to the kitchen. "And I doubt this guy is another Ted Bundy. All I know is that Blake said he met him at a release party a couple years ago and that he seemed nice. I just want to find out what he might know about the woman this morning."

"How did Blake connect the two again?" Liv called from the living room.

Laura glanced over to see her sister once again engrossed in her emails. Rockford gene indeed. "The clothes the woman was wearing. She was dressed all in vintage. Nineteen forties–era stuff."

"Interesting." Liv's attention remained on her phone screen. "So you think this has something to do with the game we just played?"

"Apparently. Maybe." Laura finished rinsing their plates then stuck them in the dishwasher. "From what I could see, there was certainly a noir vibe to how the scene was staged, and it happened at the El Cortez, one of the oldest casinos in the city." Finished with the dishes, she took a seat next to Liv again and signed back into her computer, then plugged her phone into the port and downloaded the video she'd shot earlier. "Here. See?" She pointed to the body while Liv squinted at the screen. "Look at the dress and the hair. That looks just like some of the characters we encountered in the game, right?"

Liv scrunched her nose. "You're no Spielberg, are you?"

"Just shut up and look, okay?"

"Yeah, all right," Liv said, leaning in closer and squinting. "I guess I can see a connection."

Laura minimized the game and brought up Google again. This time she typed *Vegas Noir* into her browser and scanned the pages of results. "Looks like it's still pretty popular, even though it's been around a while."

"Click on that one," Liv said, pointing to a link for a gamer forum. "Looks like it's full of juicy gossip."

They huddled together and stared at the different topics and chat rooms that popped up onscreen, many for other, more recent M Cubed games—everything from *Undead Apocalypse* to *Valhalla Vengeance.*

"Wow." Laura clicked on one thread titled Take That

Festering Flesh Fucker. "Who knew people loved blowing up zombies that much?"

"Or battling Vikings."

Laura laughed. "Those characters do look pretty hot in their horns and fur."

"Got that right, sista." Liv pointed to a small picture near the bottom of the screen. "Looks like there's a separate page for *Vegas Noir*."

"Yeah." Laura tapped the thumbnail, and a separate area opened up—a completed virtual world of old buildings and cars and men in fedoras with femme fatales draped on each arm. Glenn Miller's "In the Mood" played in the background of the fan-created realm. "This is pretty cool."

"Really detailed. Those people look almost real, don't they?"

"Kind of creepy, actually."

"Yeah, it is." Liv stretched then checked her watch and stood, shoving her phone back into her purse. "I need to get back to the office."

"And I need to get over to Turnberry Place."

"That's where he lives?"

"Yeah. The penthouse, according to Blake." Laura dug through her kitchen drawers, looking for the keycard she'd stolen from the place while covering a previous story. "It's gated. I had a lead over there a couple of years ago and accidentally kept the entry pass they gave me."

"Accidentally, huh?" Liv raised a brow at her, her expression skeptical.

"Okay. Maybe not an accident." Coming up empty, Laura tried a different drawer near the fridge. In the far corner, she spotted the dark navy plastic card. She shoved it into the outside pocket of her messenger bag. "Ready?"

"Always." Liv hooked her arm through Laura's, and they walked out the door together. Then she locked up while Liv pushed the button for the elevator. "Please promise me you won't put yourself in any danger."

Laura scoffed. "You know me."

"Yeah, I do." The elevator dinged, and they climbed in. "That's why I'm saying it."

They rode to the lobby in silence, but once the doors opened again, Laura turned to Liv and gave her a big hug. "I'll be careful. I promise. Don't work too hard, okay?"

"Too late. And look who's talking." Liv squeezed her tight then let her go. "See you Wednesday?"

"Sounds great." Laura waved as Liv headed out the entrance on the other side of the lobby and she headed out to her Impala parked along the curb. As she slid in behind the wheel and started the engine, images of the game popped back into her head, followed in short order by pictures of the man who'd invented it. Mike McQuade caused all sorts of unwanted feelings inside of her, none of which was danger.

4

———

Laura parked about a block from Turnberry Place and double-checked her makeup and hair in the rearview mirror before grabbing her messenger bag and exiting the vehicle. With luck, the same male security guard still worked here. He'd developed quite a crush on her during her visits for her last story, and he might just let her squeak past the gates, even though technically she didn't belong there.

No such luck, however, she noticed as she approached. Some big burly guy sat squished inside the tiny booth, looking sweaty and tired and completely undercompensated by the minimum-wage salary they probably paid the poor schmuck.

Ever resourceful, Laura spotted a drugstore on the other side of the street.

Ten minutes later, she was back with a plastic bag in

her hand. She strolled up to the guard station with her best flirty smile in place. Sunglasses pushed up to the top of her head, she leaned into the drive-through window of the tiny booth. "Hello, kind sir."

"Ma'am." The guard dipped the bill of his police-man-style hat, his expression stoic. "May I help you?"

"Silly me. I'm supposed to meet my friend at his apartment for dinner. I don't suppose you could let me in."

"Sorry, ma'am. No keycard, no entry."

"Oh, you mean this?" She pulled out the old keycard from her pocket and held it in front of his face.

"That's way old. They issue new ones every year. Got to have a current one."

"Damn." She winced and let her shoulders slump slightly. "He's going to be so mad."

"What's his name, ma'am? I can call and have him come down to get you here."

"Oh, no." The last thing she needed was this guy tipping off hermit McQuade that someone was looking for him. "Don't need him thinking I'm any dumber than he probably already does."

The guard gave her a side glance, his flat expression faltering. "He doesn't sound very nice if he thinks you're dumb."

Laura bit back a small smile. Maybe her flirting would pay off after all. "Oh, he's very nice. He's just really, really smart."

"Huh." The guard swiped a handkerchief across his sweaty forehead. "Whatever you say."

"You look pretty hot in there. No air conditioning?"

"None." The guy shook his head mournfully. "It's gotta be close to a hundred out today."

"Maybe this will come in handy." She raised the bag and pulled out a small desktop fan. "You want to use it?"

He started to reach for it then stopped. "What's the catch?"

"No catch." She smiled again. "You get the fan and while you're plugging it in, you might not notice me slipping inside the gates."

His dark gaze narrowed.

"Or." She shoved the fan back into the bag. "I'll just return this on my way home."

A bead of perspiration trickled down his temple, and he cursed under his breath. "Fine. But if you get caught, you're on your own, lady."

"Works for me." She handed him the bag then hustled through the small opening in the gates behind him, feeling inordinately proud of herself. She'd not only gotten what she wanted, she'd helped a guy in need. Win-win.

She strolled past the lovely fountain in the center of the plaza and wondered which building might be his. She didn't have to search long for the answer, spying two police cars parked outside the tallest building to her right. Bingo.

Slipping inside the marble lobby of the place, she stuck close to the walls to be as unobtrusive as possible. The chilly air conditioning blasted citrus-scented air through the massive space, and she located four officers, two in uniforms and two detectives, talking over by the long concierge desk. Ahead were the elevators, but without a keycard she didn't think she'd get far, and it wasn't like she could just waltz up to the desk and ask for a new one.

Against one wall she found a resident directory and scanned it fast to confirm her intel. McQuade. Penthouse.

She would've guessed the penthouse anyway, even without Blake's help, given McQuade's financial status and penchant for privacy. Great. Now all she had to do was figure out how to get up there. Maybe she could exit on one of the lower floors and take the stairs up to the top. She walked to the elevators and pressed the Up button, tapping her toes to dispel some nervous energy while she waited.

"Thank you, ma'am," one of the detectives said behind her. Footsteps echoed on the marble floors headed in her direction.

Shit.

Laura ducked her head and turned, feigning deep interest in the potted plant in front of her as the detectives headed toward the elevators. The uniformed officers still stood near the entrance. She inched closer to the two men nearest her, hoping she might garner some tidbits of their conversation.

"You got a hot date this weekend?" one guy said.

"Nah. Going out with Gigi from the Tropicana again. You?"

"My wife's in charge of all my hot dates now, man."

"Right."

The elevator dinged and a man stepped out, stopping abruptly as the two officers stepped in front of him. "Mr. McQuade?"

Laura glanced over and caught the man's gaze—intelligent, guarded, sexy as hell.

She looked away fast, heat storming her cheeks. He didn't know her from Adam, yet she got the distinct impression he saw right through her, saw that she didn't belong here. Her pulse thudded loud in her ears, blocking out the voices around her. She needed to hear what they were saying, needed to get her lead, get her story.

Calm down, idiot.

After a deep, steadying breath, Laura eased closer still to the small group of men.

"I'm Detective Hopkins and this is Detective Ruiz. We're from the Metro homicide division, and we'd like to ask you some questions, if you have a few moments."

"What's happened?" McQuade asked, his voice deeper, rougher than she'd imagined. Velvet over gravel.

Definitely not geeky gamer. "Have I done something wrong?"

"No, no, Mr. McQuade." One of the detectives gestured toward a small seating area to Laura's left. "We just have a few questions for you regarding one of the video games your company produces."

"Oh."

Through her lashes, she watched McQuade shove his hands deeper into the pockets of his navy blue hoodie and nod. He walked toward the seating area and caught her eye once more. A spark passed between them before vanishing so fast she wondered if it had even happened at all.

Laura looked from him to the elevator and saw the doors still open, waiting, as if beckoning her forward. Behind her, the men took a seat.

"This morning, Mr. McQuade," Detective Hopkins said, "we found the body of a Barbara Newton in the pool at the El Cortez Hotel."

Barbara Newton.

Now she had a name to go with the corpse she'd seen earlier. She could get the rest from Troy later. Right now she had a penthouse to investigate, and with McQuade's back to the elevators and his attention on the cops, this was a perfect opportunity. Fists clenched, she walked over and stepped inside the elevator. As soon as she pressed the P button for penthouse, the doors slid closed, and her tense shoulders relaxed slightly.

Okay, Laura. You've got this.

She swiped the old keycard through the slot near the penthouse button and waited, hoping maybe they changed cards but not codes.

Nothing.

Tried again.

No movement.

One more swipe.

Nada.

Dammit. She shoved the card back into her pocket as the doors slid open again then she stepped off, only to find herself face to face with Mike McQuade himself— all dark stubble and even darker secrets. Her heartbeat doubled as she fought to remain calm.

A slight quirk crossed his full lips, not quite a smile and not quite a frown, but about halfway between, if that were possible. A fresh wave of adrenaline sizzled through her veins. Whatever that look was on his face, it suggested he knew exactly what she was up to.

Laura lifted her chin slightly and attempted to step around him. Except he stepped the same way and they collided again, his hard-muscled chest pressing into her. She swallowed hard, mumbled an apology and stepped the other way. He did the same.

Finally, she looked up to see him grinning down at her as if he knew something she didn't. Which, if he were the killer, he probably did. She cleared the sudden constriction from her throat and forced words past her tight vocal cords. "Sorry."

He stared at her. "Can I help you?"

More than you know.

"I'm on my way out." She sidled around him again, but he caught her arm.

"You new to this building?"

Crap.

"I've been staying with friends."

"Oh. Been here long, then?"

"Long enough." She tried to pull free but couldn't. "Why?"

His previously friendly grin turned frigid. "Because I'd like to know what the hell you're doing on this elevator."

GROUPIE, *had to be.*

Except this one didn't look like his typical fangirl— she was far prettier than most, with an intelligent gleam in her gorgeous hazel eyes. Still, as intriguing as this little sneak was, that didn't mean he'd let his guard down any time soon. He'd been obsessively stalked one too many times to let that happen.

When she didn't respond, Mike looked her up and down, squeezing her arm a tad tighter—not hard enough to hurt but hard enough to let her know he meant business. "I'll ask you one more time, then I'll hail one of those detectives if I don't like your answer. What are you doing in this elevator? It's private for the condos on the top three floors and I think I'd remember if you were a regular visitor to any of my neighbors."

Her gaze narrowed slightly, and the pink in her creamy cheeks blossomed higher. Feisty. And if there was one thing he dug in a woman, it was feistiness. He might live like a paranoid monk these days, but that didn't mean he didn't notice an attractive woman.

"Look, Mr. McQuade, this isn't what you think," she said, her voice a tad huskier. With tension or attraction, he wasn't sure. Either way, it didn't much matter. He steered clear of most all relationships these days, romantic or otherwise. Some called him cutthroat, some called him secretive. They were both wrong. What he had was a plan for his future success, and it didn't involve socializing. Socializing led to entanglements, and entanglements led to people getting too close and getting hurt. He couldn't allow that to happen again. These days, it was up to him to control the hurt.

He waited for her to continue.

She kept her gaze locked with his, an odd mix of confidence and obvious fluster. Quick on her feet, too. He'd have to be careful with this one. She gestured with her free hand toward the seating area he'd just vacated. "It looked like you were having a private conversation and I didn't want to intrude, so I thought I'd wait for you upstairs, but I don't have the right keycard."

Wait for me upstairs?

Mike exhaled and did his best to keep his expression stoic despite the kick in his pulse. His agenda was free this afternoon. No appointments. No meetings. And no one from the guards' station had contacted him to clear her presence. Which meant she must've conned them somehow. He added crafty to her growing list of attributes. Mike decided to play along just for the pleasure of seeing her talk her way out of it. "So you're here to see me, huh? Why? I thought you said you were staying with friends."

"I'm Laura Rockford." She extended her free hand toward him. "I'm...uh...doing a documentary featuring icons of the gaming world. My assistant was supposed to contact you, but based on this conversation, I'm assuming he didn't. Sorry about that whole business about staying with friends. I didn't realize that was you, just figured you were some creep."

He frowned. That name sounded familiar. "Rockford? As in Rockford Security?"

"Yes. My older brother Blake runs the company." She smiled politely. "He mentioned meeting you at a release party for one of your games a couple of years ago."

"Did he?" Seems half the people in Vegas had met him at some such party or another over the years, but he really had met Blake. Used him for security, in fact. Still, the connection between the woman in front of him and his security firm did little to ease his anxiety or his suspicions.

As if sensing his discomfort with her disclosure, Laura was quick to add, "But that's my brother. I'm not involved in his company at all. I strictly make documentaries."

"Name some of your work."

Her eyes widened slightly, and she glanced away. Most people might not have noticed her gestures, at least on a conscious level, but Mike wasn't most people. He'd spent years studying human interactions and physiological cues to make the characters in his games as realistic as possible. Based on her actions, she was definitely hiding something.

"Well." She shuffled from foot to foot and bit her full lower lip. Mike clenched his hand to keep from reaching out and rubbing the pad of his thumb over the abraded area. "This will be my first big feature. I just graduated from NYU last year." She glanced up at him as if gauging his reaction. "But I promise, this is all legit and will be handled with the utmost care and professionalism."

The doors to his elevator remained open, and across the hall, the two detectives still lingered, glancing in his direction every so often.

He let Laura's arm go and crossed his instead. Her tale had gotten so elaborate, he wondered how she'd be able to keep all the strings of her deceit web straight, but it was like watching a horrific train crash. He couldn't look away. And he couldn't stop. Not yet. "Tell me more."

A slow smile spread across her pretty face, and Mike's blood pulsed thick in his veins. She was dangerous, in more ways than just her snooping. Still, he knew Blake Rockford and, more importantly, he trusted him. A rare and valuable commodity in his world. If this was his sister, then perhaps he could trust her as well, to a certain extent. He'd know more after he ran a background search on her later. "My plan is to expose the true genius behind today's bestselling video games."

"I don't do interviews." The less his fans knew about the kind of man he really was, the better. "Sorry."

"This isn't your typical interview, I swear. And it won't take long at all. Having you as part of my film could make it a real contender at next year's Sundance Festival. Please." She placed a hand on his forearm and blinked up at him with her soulful, Disney-princess eyes, and Mike felt his stalwart barriers fracturing.

Dammit. He couldn't deal with this. Not today. But now that she'd met him and knew where he lived, he doubted she'd give up so easily. Maybe it would be to his advantage to play along, at least for a little while longer. That way he could keep control of her and the situation. "I don't have time right now."

"That's fine. I've got another appointment too. How about I come back tomorrow at this same time? Would that work for you, Mr. McQuade?"

"Fine." He stepped back inside his elevator, and she stepped out into the lobby. Mike swiped his keycard through the slot then jabbed the button for his penthouse before stuffing the thing back into the pocket of his favorite navy hoodie. "See you tomorrow, then."

The doors shut on her smiling face, and his heart sank as the elevator rose.

Keeping Laura Rockford close would be either a brilliant idea or a spectacular failure. Between her lies and his reactions, one thing was for sure. His well-controlled life had just become a hell of a lot more chaotic. And interesting.

5

———

Laura arrived back at Turnberry Place the following day promptly at four p.m. The heavy gear bag made her arm ache as she waited at the front guard station while they called in her arrival to Mike McQuade. She hadn't gotten much sleep the night before, instead staying up far too late playing *Vegas Noir* to discover all the intricacies of his imaginary world. At least, that's what she told herself. Truth was, the game was fun. And addictive.

So, bleary eyed and irritable, she'd spent her morning in her small cubicle at the *Chronicle* offices, taking care of weekly paperwork and doing a bit of research into Barbara Newton, the murder victim from the day before. Unfortunately, there were what seemed like a million Barbara Newtons on Facebook, and without anything more to go on but a name, she had no idea which one was correct.

Afterward, she'd dug out an old camcorder and tripod from one of the newspaper's supply closets. She stuffed them into a dusty duffle bag she'd found alongside and headed back to the police station, hoping Troy might feed her a bit more information about the evidence found at the El Cortez.

But he hadn't had much to tell her either, even though she'd bribed him with yet another double espresso and triple-fudge brownie. He'd been going over the security footage, or lack thereof, from the historic hotel from the time of the murder. The footage had been a bust. Nothing but blank tape, due to the ancient cameras at the El Cortez, Troy assured her. Not tampering. The only thing of value she'd discovered had been that the victim had been stabbed. Once. Through the heart. Just like in level three of Mike's game. The police were still searching for the weapon used.

So here she was now, again passing through the gates of the Turnberry with what seemed like a thousand pounds of gear and untruths weighing her down. She didn't like to lie. Truth was in her nature. But when it came to getting what she knew could be a career-making story from a guy who never gave interviews, Laura did what was necessary.

This time when she entered the spacious marble lobby of Mike's building, she walked directly up to the concierge desk as she'd been instructed by the guard at the station outside and was handed a green plastic keycard by the gal behind the counter. "You'll find the elevators right over there, Ms. Rockford. Just swipe the card in the slot beneath the button and press P for penthouse."

"Thanks." Laura hoisted her heavy bag higher in her grip and headed for the site of her run-in with Mike McQuade the day before. He was far from what she'd expected—much more handsome and closed off in person. He'd be a tough nut to crack, but she'd broken tougher.

The doors dinged open, and she stepped aboard the elevator then swiped the card. Soon, the car jerked upward toward the top floor of the building. She wondered what kind of lifestyle a guy like McQuade preferred. He was young—only three years older than her—richer than King Midas and smart as sin. Hell, his place probably looked like a set straight out of the *Matrix*.

She chuckled as the car bumped to a halt and the doors opened once more, this time revealing a bright, airy lobby with floor-to-ceiling windows on one side displaying fantastic views of the Strip beyond. There was also a man waiting for her—shorter, unassuming, painfully awkward.

Not Mike. And definitely not the *Matrix* either.

Unsure what to say, she gave the man a polite smile.

"Um, hi. My name's Laura Rockford. I have a four o'clock meeting with Mr. McQuade."

"Hi," the man said curtly and gestured for her to follow him into the penthouse proper. He was dressed similar to the way Mike had been the day before in a T-shirt, hoodie, and jeans. The embroidered horse logo on the front of the sweatshirt told her his apparel wasn't inexpensive, as did his top-of-the-line sneakers.

"Are you a friend of Mr. McQuade?" she asked.

"Mike should be out in a minute." He pointed to one of the armchairs in the sprawling living room in what she assumed was a gesture for her to sit and wait.

All righty then. Laura took a seat and continued to watch the guy from beneath her lashes. He moved around the place like he was comfortable being there, so maybe he was part of the cleaning crew or a personal assistant? The latter seemed more likely, given his wardrobe. Or...

She eyed the man closer. Maybe Mike McQuade wasn't into women.

Just because she'd felt definite flutters the previous day didn't mean he had. And this apparently mute guy who'd escorted her in seemed fine walking into another room beyond and settling in behind what appeared to be a wall of computer monitors and equipment. Far too comfortable for a mere personal assistant.

"Ah, Miss Rockford." Mike entered the living room through yet another door on the other side of the room.

From what she could see, his penthouse took up the entire top floor of the building, meaning it was massive. "Security said you were on your way up." He walked past the guy on his computer system in the other room without a glance, instead riffling through some papers in his hand. "You're on time. I like people who don't waste mine."

She bit back the snarky retort hovering on her tongue at his pompous tone and pasted on an accommodating smile instead.

Get the story. Get the story. Get the story.

The story was the most important thing here, not the fact McQuade spoke to her with the same level of enthusiasm normally reserved for unpleasant things found stuck on bottoms of shoes.

"Thanks for inviting me here today." Laura glanced over at the guy in the room again. "Your friend was kind enough to let me in."

"Oh, uh. Yeah. Excuse me a sec." A small muscle ticced near McQuade's tight jaw as he leaned into the other room, tossing the papers in his hand to the guy. "Hey, Ted. The idea of having those combo accelerators for experienced players is good, but I don't want to shut out first-time or casual players who don't have as much skill either. What if we made a tutorial or journal entry for the combos so anyone who wanted to study them could figure it out? And how about we make them less of a necessity to beat the bosses and more of a bonus?

Extra XP or a buff to health or reduced cooldown times?"

From what Laura could see, the other guy didn't look happy about the suggested changes. In fact, given his gloomy expression, he looked downright pissed. So this guy wasn't an assistant or a lover. He was one of Mike's programmers. Laura filed the information, along with the guy's name, in her mental databanks.

After a few tense seconds, Ted gave Mike a grim nod then turned back to his screens, shoulders hunched. Apparently all was not sunshine and rainbows in Mike's little tech world.

Mike closed the door on the guy and faced Laura once more. "Shall we get started? I've got a lot of work to get done yet tonight."

"Oh, sure." She set her messenger bag aside and started setting up the tripod and camcorder while he pulled out his phone. "Do you work from home a lot?"

"Sometimes." Mike seemed completely absorbed by whatever he was doing on his device and didn't bother to look at her as he answered. "Depends on the day."

The door to the room beyond opened and Ted slumped out, head down, his voice low as his gaze darted between the two of them. "I'll finish up at Corporate, if that's okay."

"Okay, see ya." Mike waved him off, his attention still focused on his phone.

Laura finished loading a small tape into the camera

then took a seat on the chair and waited for Mike to notice her again. She took the opportunity to get a feel for his personal style. Everything in his home was crisp and clean, the décor in neutral shades of beige and off-white. Not exactly the post-apocalyptic gloom and doom she'd been expecting. The furniture was mainly leather or microfiber and overstuffed, giving the place a comfortable vibe. At least the parts she could see.

Curiosity piqued but not comfortable asking for a full tour, she relied on the next best thing. "Um, I'm a little thirsty after lugging all this gear from my car. Could I maybe have a glass of water or something?"

"Kitchen's through there." He hiked his chin toward the far corner of the room. Again, no eye contact. "Glasses are in the cabinet by the sink."

"Thanks." She stood and walked into a spacious chef's kitchen, done in warm granite and gleaming stainless steel. This place would've been Martha Stewart's dream. She chuckled as she headed toward the cabinet he'd indicated and reached inside for a large tumbler. After filling it with cold water from the tap, she leaned her hips against the countertop, surveying the rest of the space. No clutter, no dirty dishes, the complete opposite of her place. A large island stood in the center of the space, with a second built-in sink and storage space underneath. She spotted a manila folder lying near one corner.

One quick peek couldn't hurt anything. After a quick

glance to ensure Mike was still occupied with whatever he was doing on his phone, Laura pulled the file closer with one finger. Flipped the cover open and covered her mouth as her breath caught in her chest. Good thing she hadn't taken another drink, because it would've spewed over everything.

Inside were photos—various shots from the *Vegas Noir* video game, all of the same victim and death scene at the El Cortez. They were the same caliber of shots the police investigators usually got, extreme close-ups, lots of details. A small logo marked one corner of each photo. FG and a copyright mark. On the back was stamped a name—Felicia Gomez.

Holy shit.

"You find everything okay?" Mike asked, walking in then stopping abruptly. His expression darkened to a scowl, and his brown gaze hardened as he took in the open folder and the papers in her hand. "Yeah. I can see you have."

Stunned, both by what she'd just seen and by the fact she'd gotten caught, Laura remained silent as he stalked over and snatched the folder and its contents from her then tossed them in a nearby trash can. "Forget these. One of my more crazed fans sent them over. Are you ready for the interview?"

Hands shaky, she set her glass down and nodded. "Doesn't receiving graphic stuff like that bother you?"

"Occupational hazard," he mumbled as he led her

back out into the sunny living room. They took seats across from each other, and she pulled her trusty notebook from her messenger bag, glad for the distraction of the questions she'd prepared in advance. Her sister's words from the day before rang through her head.

You can't just walk into a killer's home and accuse him of murder...

Maybe not, but she could at least gather some more intel on the elusive Mike McQuade. Her instincts told her he knew more about those damned pictures she'd found than he was letting on, and she had every intention of finding out exactly what.

But first she had to get him to relax, open up, trust her. Okay, maybe the last one was a long shot, but a girl had to try. She pressed Record on the camera and ran a finger down the list in front of her. "Thanks so much for agreeing to speak with me, Mr. McQuade. Why don't we start off with you telling me a little bit about yourself?"

He exhaled, long and slow, as if he were facing a firing squad not a video camera. "My name's Mike McQuade. I'm the president and CEO of M Cubed Games. We've been in business for ten years, and we are the premier developer, marketer, publisher, and distributor of video RPGs in the United States."

His somewhat stodgy demeanor lightened a bit as he discussed his business, a flicker of passion and pride glowing in his soft brown eyes. For a moment, Laura couldn't help wondering what other activities might elicit that same response. *Dinner? A good movie?* She shook her head to clear the fuzzy, seductive images of her and Mike curled up on the couch together and forced herself to focus on the task at hand. "Are you from Las Vegas originally?"

"Yep, I'm a Sin City boy, born and bred."

"Do you have family here?"

He clasped his hands across his flat stomach and smiled—a rare sight that nearly stole her breath—all sweetness and pure affection. "Three siblings. Two older, Sean and Jenna, and my youngest sister, Reba. And my parents, of course."

She couldn't help grinning along with him. Family was everything. "You sound pretty close."

"Yeah. My oldest brother is in programming too. He's a software developer in Silicon Valley, God help him. Not that the distance stops him from trying to oversee all of our lives." He snorted and shook his head. "And my older sister's also in California, but she's getting her PhD in law from Stanford. So now it's just Reba and me left here. She's the baby of our group and quite a handful, but I do the best I can."

"Right." Laura laughed, all too familiar with nosy older brothers and their interfering ways. "Your oldest sounds like Blake. Talk about mother hen syndrome."

"I know, right?" He tilted his head and narrowed his gaze. "What about you?"

"What about me?"

"You've got a pretty big clan yourself, don't you?"

"Yeah, there's six of us Rockford kids, plus Mom and Dad."

"Must get pretty crazy around the holidays."

"You have no idea."

They laughed, and for the first time in a long time, Laura felt completely comfortable with a man who wasn't a member of her family. She leaned forward in her chair. "Where'd you graduate high school?"

He scoffed and leaned forward as well. "Las Vegas High. Go Wildcats!"

"Me too."

"It's the only place to go."

"Totally." She sat back and noticed his coffee cup on the table. "You like 1020 Café too? Over by the Mob Museum on Stewart Street?"

"Love it." He picked up the cup and turned it to gaze at the logo. "Not sure why they picked that location though. But I'm officially addicted to their espresso. Get one almost every morning. Can't think straight without it. Why?"

"I'm surprised I haven't seen you in there since I'm a regular too."

"Huh." He checked his watch. "Damn. I'm really sorry, but I've got another meeting shortly."

"Oh. Sure. No problem." Laura reached over and switched off the camera then started to gather her things. It didn't even occur to her until she was taking down the tripod that she hadn't asked him anything about the victim or those disturbing pictures she'd found in his kitchen. "Hey, I've, uh, actually played *Vegas Noir* a couple of times as research for this interview. Those pictures in the kitchen reminded me of your game."

"Yeah." Mike ran a hand through his short, thick brown hair. One errant curl fell over his forehead, and she battled the urge to stroke it back into place. "There are some real sickos out there. I hate that someone would use my creations for something so heinous, but crazy people do crazy things, I guess. Forget those pictures. They're not a big deal."

"Yeah, I guess." *Not a big deal.* Like she'd stumbled on rotten bananas instead of candid photos of a dead woman. His words left her cold. She zipped the tripod and camera back into their duffle then hung her messenger bag across her body and hoisted the heavy bag in her hand once more. "Thanks again for your time today."

"My pleasure." He placed a hand against the small of her back to lead her to the elevators, and her breath hitched. He handed her a business card with his contact information then pressed the button for her. "Be careful going home."

"I will, thanks." She bounced on the balls of her feet to relieve some of her pent-up nervous tension. "And I'll call you if I need anything else. For the documentary, of course."

"Of course." The elevator dinged and he helped her on, then leaned an arm against the door frame, gifting her with another of his rare smiles. "I look forward to talking to you again, Laura Rockford. For the documentary."

"Of course."

As she descended back to ground level, Laura slumped against the wall of the elevator and cringed, mortified. She'd flirted with the guy. How lame could she get? She was not a flirter. And Lord knew she had no business even considering a date with Mike McQuade. He was her story. And until said story was done, she couldn't lose her impartiality.

It would be bad for her career.

It would be bad for her life goals.

But most of all, she feared it would be very, very bad for her jaded, cautious heart.

***

HOURS LATER, Mike stood on the balcony of his penthouse and stared at the glittering lights of Vegas below. The interview with Laura Rockford had gotten so far out of control he needed an atlas to show him the way back. No matter how attractive she was, he had no business handing out details about his family like cheap Halloween candy. No matter how easy it was to talk to her. No matter how much they seemed to have in common.

Especially after what had happened with his baby sister.

So what if they both came from big families? Who cared if they both had bossy older brothers who lived to dictate the lives of their siblings, with loving intentions, of course. And what did it matter if they'd both use their smarts to advance their pursuits, no matter the costs.

So many similarities, yet still worlds apart.

God, Blake Rockford's younger sister. Here, in his penthouse, snooping around in his life. He still remembered the night he and Blake had met. The release party for *Vegas Noir*. The evening that had changed Mike's life forever. And not in the way he'd expected.

Someone had died that night too.

An involuntary shiver ran through him, and he turned his back on the dazzling panorama before him.

No. It was best to forget any ideas about Laura Rockford beyond the professional.

He stayed solitary for a reason.

Not to mention she'd lied to him. His background check on her had proved quite enlightening. Turned out she was a features reporter for the *Chronicle*, not a documentary filmmaker. Made him feel more than justified in installing the tracking software on her phone when she'd been here earlier. All she'd had to do was get within the vicinity of his Wi-Fi network and voila. App installed. Now he could track her movements across all of his network devices—mobile, tablet, laptop. Whenever, wherever. Anytime she accessed the Internet, he could determine her location. Just one more safeguard in his already well-armored life. Laura Rockford was up to something other than wanting a documentary and it was prudent to keep an eye on her in order to figure out what it was.

His phone beeped, and he pulled it from his pocket, staring down at the screen and snorting. *Hello, butterfly, welcome to my web.*

Apparently Laura had gone home after their interview, as she'd claimed. Or at least he assumed it was her home, since the address belonged to an upscale downtown apartment complex not far from his own place. He'd run the address to be sure later.

Why had he been so careless, leaving those pictures out for her to find? Then again, he wasn't used to having people around. Well, anyone other than Ted, who didn't really count since he was the only person Mike knew who was more secretive than himself. Hell, that guy made him look like a frigging blabbermouth.

And speaking of those photos. He'd fished them from the trash can after Laura had left and locked them up in the safe in his bedroom until he had time to deal with the culprit.

Felicia Gomez.

Another obsessed fangirl he'd met a few years ago at

one of the rare gamer conventions he'd actually attended. Even in his carefully planned disguise, she'd recognized him, following him around with her high-pitched, squeaky voice, showing him all of her artwork based on his video games.

Most people considered her a kook, an erratic loony who maybe got a little too lost in the fantasy worlds she loved. But Mike had seen that glint of determination in her eyes, that spark of crazed willfulness that told him she'd do anything to get what she wanted. And what she wanted was Mike to create a game just for her, to make her the star of her own virtual world. A queen of her own make-believe universe.

Her artist's touch was all over those prints from the kitchen—the bold brushstrokes, the delicate use of color, the slight nod to his original with a few minor tweaks to make it all her own. Not to mention her copyright in the corner and her name stamped on the back. Seems Felicia had gotten bolder since their last run-in, no longer trying to hide her insanity.

His phone beeped once more, and he looked down to see Laura was on the move again. Now at the 1020 Café. He hadn't been lying when he'd said he was addicted to that place. Their espressos had quickly become his drug of choice. The fact she loved the place too meant she had good taste to go along with her intelligence. Another mark in her pros column.

Then the dot marking her position moved once

more, down about a block to the nearby 18B Galleries. The momentary warmth in his chest cooled with dread.

Felicia Gomez had a studio there.

He glanced at his watch. After nine now.

Shit.

Why the hell couldn't Laura Rockford stay at home and eat ice cream and watch reruns like a normal person?

Reluctantly, he pulled on his hoodie and added a pair of sunglasses despite the late hour and the heat then headed for the door. Given the nature of Felicia's photos and Laura Rockford's inclination for meddling, he shuddered to think what might happen if those two connected.

Didn't matter. He intended to do whatever was in his power to make sure that didn't happen.

6

———

Laura weaved through the nighttime crowds on Main Street, headed for 18B, near the corner of Charleston Avenue. She hadn't planned on going back out tonight, but once she'd pulled up the website for the artist listed on those photos in Mike's apartment, she couldn't resist. From what she'd found during her Internet search, the woman had a studio right here in Las Vegas and one favorite subject matter—Mike McQuade.

What she couldn't decide until she met the woman in person was whether she was a wickedly devoted fan or psychopathic serial killer. From the graphic depictions in those photos and their eerie resemblance to the crime scene at the El Cortez, Laura tended to lean toward the latter at this point. Now, if she could just convince J.J., her editor at the paper, to let her continue investigating what she knew deep inside would be a big story. Possibly the biggest story to hit the *Chronicle*'s front page in decades.

And of course, Mike acted like those pictures weren't any big deal, said he got them all the time, said for her to forget about them. *As if.* If he received awful stuff like that in his mail routinely and wasn't bothered by it, then he was either more disturbed than she'd suspected or he and this artist were in cahoots.

Or both.

Neither option helped relieve the niggle of unease that had bored into her belly at first sight of those photos. Half a block from her destination, Laura pulled out her phone and hit the speed dial button for J.J.'s extension. He answered on the second ring.

"This better be good, Rockford. You know my rule about work calls after nine p.m."

She feigned surprise. "Oh dear, is it that late already?"

"You've got thirty seconds, Rockford."

"Fine." She sidled around a group of college kids laughing and smoking in the middle of the sidewalk. "Listen, I'm pretty sure I'm sitting on a big lead. Huge. Front-page stuff."

"Go on." The sloth-like tone of her editor's voice said he found the proposition doubtful. "Twenty-five."

"You know that murder at the El Cortez pool yesterday?"

"Twenty."

"The one with the woman in vintage clothes. Davis covered it this morning."

"Fifteen. Barbara Newton. Kids finishing high school in the spring, off to college in the fall. Father died five years ago. Sad and tragic, blah, blah, blah."

"Your compassion is underwhelming." Laura stopped outside a gallery on the corner of Main and Charleston. A large graphic, grinning skull had been painted on one side of the building in neon-bright shades of orange, green, and yellow. She double-checked the address to be sure. Yep. This was it. "And it gets better."

"Five seconds left. Make it good."

"I think Mike McQuade might have something to do with the murder."

Silence.

Laura held the phone away from her ear and checked to see if she'd lost service. "You still there, J.J.?"

"What makes you think the local tech mogul had anything to do with some woman getting stabbed near Fremont Street?"

"The crime scene. The way everything was staged to look exactly like something in one of his video games. The fact he had pictures from some artist in his kitchen that looked exactly like what I saw near that pool yesterday."

"Wait a minute. You were in McQuade's apartment? When?" Her editor's tone shifted from boredom to intrigue. "The guy's practically a hermit, from what I hear."

Laura grinned. "I got skills, what can I say? I spent the afternoon today interviewing him."

"No shit?" J.J. actually sounded impressed. No easy feat for a guy who'd cut his journalistic teeth on Watergate. "You get anything out of him?"

"Enough to make me think this could be front-page stuff. I'm telling you, J.J., this guy's hiding something. I feel it in my gut. I'm standing outside the artist's studio now, about to go in and talk to her regarding those photos I found in Mike's kitchen."

"Does he know you found them?"

She swallowed hard. "Yeah. He walked in on me looking at them."

"What'd he do?"

"Threw them in the trash and told me to forget about them."

J.J. exhaled loud. "I don't know, Rockford. McQuade's got a lot of money and backing in the local community. If you're wrong about him, this could cost you your job. Mine too, if we're not careful."

"I'm always careful, J.J." She tapped the toe of her sneaker against the pavement. "C'mon. Do I have the green light to go ahead with this investigation or not? Think of the prestige, the awards, the—"

"Lawsuits?" J.J.'s muffled curse echoed through the line. "What about that piece you've got due at the end of the week? The one about the old lady turning one hundred and five?"

"I'll get that done too. Promise."

Another hesitation.

Laura's hopes lived and died in those short seconds.

"Fine. Send me what you've got and I'll take a look. But I'm telling you, Rockford." The warning in his tone sent a fresh wave of adrenaline pumping through her system. "You so much as step a hair over the line on this one and I'll stick you in the mailroom for the rest of your natural-born life. The only byline you'll see will be at the grocery store checkout. Got it?"

"Yes, sir." She couldn't stop grinning despite the serious task ahead of her. "I'll email my research right now."

After ending the call, Laura typed in a quick email to J.J. and attached both the grainy video she'd shot at the El Cortez crime scene plus links to the Internet pages about McQuade and his company and his games, as well as information on the artist she was going to visit now. Once she was finished, she shoved the phone back into her messenger bag, smoothed her hands down the thighs of her jeans, then headed inside the gallery.

What she saw inside took her breath away. From the images on Felicia Gomez's website, she knew the woman was obsessed with *Vegas Noir*, but nothing like this. Every single five-by-five image on every single wall was from Mike's 1940s imaginary universe, all of various crime scenes from the game, including the one she'd visited the day before. People milled about and discussed the artworks like they were looking at still-life veggies and not dead bodies. Except they weren't actual dead bodies. Upon inspection, Laura could tell they were models, posed to look like the scenes from the game dressed in vintage clothing and with antique props. The whole thing was a bit too bizarre and surreal for Laura's taste.

Somewhat disgusted, she stepped up to the closest image and studied it carefully. A close-up shot of the widow's body near the pool. The muted grays and blacks of the background only served to highlight the red of her dress, making it seem almost as shocking as the pool of blood beneath the victim's chest. She leaned in closer and squinted. The blood spread pattern was the same as what she'd witnessed at the El Cortez, but the body's position was slightly different. At the actual crime scene, the widow's hands had been loose at her sides, palm open and up as if in supplication. Here, the hands were clasped at her waist. Laura started to take her phone out again. She would need to compare the actual video to be sure, but this looked like a damned close match.

"I'm sorry." A pretty African-American woman with curly brown hair and light mocha skin stepped in beside her. "No photos, please. There are thumbnails on my website of this collection, though, if you're interested in buying. I make smaller versions too."

"Oh." Laura slid her phone back into her bag and

flashed her best engaging smile. Felicia Gomez was younger than she'd expected—maybe mid-twenties—and didn't seem crazy. Not yet anyway. She played dumb to see what new information she might glean. "Are you the artist?"

"I am." She extended a hand. Long, slim fingers. Delicate and nimble. The hands of an artist. Or a murderer. "Felicia Gomez."

"Laura Rockford." She turned back to the artwork. "You seem pretty inspired by the subject matter."

"Hell yeah. *Vegas Noir* is my life." Felicia's smile grew a tad wider. "I just love the whole world, the grittiness of it, how real it all seems, the attention to detail. There's nothing else like it out there."

"Do you know the creator?"

"Mike McQuade?" Felicia's smile faltered. "Yeah, I know him."

"He commissioned these works from you?" Laura glanced sideways at Felicia, trying to gauge her reaction.

"Uh, no. How cool would that be though?" Her expression turned wistful, with just a hint of irritation. "No, I did these on my own. I sent him copies of my work once. But all that got me was a restraining order."

"Restraining order?" Laura added that information to her growing list of things to ask Troy about on her next trip to the station. "Over some pictures? Seems a bit extreme."

"It was a big misunderstanding." Felicia gave a dismissive wave. "No big deal."

No big deal. That was the second time she'd heard that phrase today, and it didn't sit any better with her now than it had then. These callous people might not consider the lost life of one woman earthshaking, but Laura wasn't about to let this victim's death go unavenged.

Still, she needed more to go on if she was going to turn this into the breaking news phenomenon she'd promised her editor. So she pushed her feelings aside and pressed on for more details. "You're a superfan of this game then, huh?"

Felicia chuckled. "Yeah, I guess you could call me that." She looked Laura up and down. "You ever played?"

"Me? Nah. No time." *Lie.*

"You should. Best RPG out there."

"RPG?"

"Role-playing game. You immerse yourself in the world, become your character. It's amazing. Like having a whole other second virtual life that no one knows about. You can be anyone. Do anything."

"Anything, huh?" She glanced between the artwork and Felicia. "Maybe I should try it sometime. What happens, though, when playing in the virtual world isn't enough anymore?"

"What do you mean?"

"Like your pictures. Seems like maybe you've taken this virtual world and brought it into the real one."

"It happens sometimes." Felicia nodded. "I admit when I took these shots, I really felt like I'd entered the game, you know? Like I was a part of it all. Even though, technically, some of the characters I portray are men in the game."

"But you aren't in *Vegas Noir*."

"No." Felicia tilted her head at Laura. "You're right. I'm not. No matter how bad I want to be."

The air practically sizzled with tension as she asked the question that had plagued her since she'd first walked in the door. "Is that why you took it to the next level?"

"I'm sorry?" Felicia took a step back and crossed her arms. "I don't understand."

"The murder yesterday. The widow at the El Cortez."

Another step back. Felicia's friendly smile dissolved into a frown. "What?"

"A woman was killed yesterday near the pool at the El Cortez Hotel. The crime scene was staged almost exactly like your photo here."

Felicia's brown eyes widened. "Oh my God. That's why you're here? You think I had something to do with that?" She held up her hands and took another small step away. "Listen, I take the pictures, but I would never, ever kill someone."

Laura narrowed her gaze, taking note of Felicia's

retreating body position and horrified expression. "Then it looks like there's an even bigger fan of the game out there than you."

"What are you, a cop or something?"

"Or something." Laura took off toward the door, calling out over her shoulder. "Watch yourself, Ms. Gomez. I will be."

She pushed out into the warm night and walked several feet away from the door before leaning against the wall to catch her breath. One more suspect down and a boatload of unanswered questions. At least she knew Mike hadn't commissioned those god-awful shots. Somehow that made her feel better, even though she knew her growing attraction to him was a definite no-no. Hardcore journalists did not fall for their subjects.

After a deep breath, she stepped away from the gallery and headed back to her car. Laura had almost reached the corner when she stopped in her tracks. A silhouette stood beneath the streetlight near her Impala —tall, broad shoulders, navy hoodie. Her heart stumbled before racing ahead in triple time.

Mike.

Shit.

Nervous butterflies tickled through her stomach at the sight of him. She tried to flip her hair over her shoulder in the same confident way Liv did and tripped over her own feet in the process.

Smooth move, dumbass.

Laura recovered her balance and glanced away from Mike's direct stare. He hadn't looked away from her once in what seemed like her long journey to reach him, although it couldn't have been more than a dozen steps. His full lips were compressed into a thin, white line, and his expression appeared decidedly stern.

"I thought you were going home after our interview." His words emerged more growl than speech.

"And I thought you had a lot of work to do tonight." She clicked the button on her key fob to unlock the Impala then opened the passenger side and tossed her messenger bag onto the seat. "Since when are my plans any of your business, Mr. McQuade?"

"Since you're nosing around in places where you shouldn't be, Ms. Rockford." He yanked the car door from her grasp and slammed it shut then leaned against it so she couldn't open it again. "You shouldn't be down here."

"Why not? Last time I checked, it was still a free country." She started to walk toward the driver's side, but he grabbed her arm and stopped her. She gave him a pointed stare, dropping her gaze to his grip then looking back to his eyes. "Take your hands off me."

"Or what?"

"Or I'll make sure you walk funny for a week."

His tense shoulders relaxed a bit, and a small smile now played around his firm lips. She briefly wondered if said lips would feel as soft as they looked before shoving the crazy notion aside. She had no business thinking about his lips. None.

He released her. "Fine."

"Fine." She crossed her arms and held her ground despite the fact she stood close enough to him now to feel his heat through her thin cotton top, to smell his scent—cedar and musk and something else, something indefinably him. A breeze had kicked up tonight, and though the temperatures were still high, a slight shiver ran through her. He raised a speculative brow, as if he knew damned well the effect he had on her. To distract herself from her thudding pulse, she concentrated on business. "Why shouldn't I be down here?"

"Did you see Felicia?"

Well, then. So much for subtlety. "Maybe."

"Don't lie to me. I saw you come out of her gallery."

"Why'd you bother asking me then?" She leaned her hip against the car as well. "Seems you have all the answers, don't you Mr. McQuade?"

"Mike."

"What?"

"After the interview this afternoon, I think we should be on a first-name basis. Call me Mike."

Better than the alternative, she supposed, which wasn't nice or even printable. The guy riled her up without even trying, in ways she didn't even want to think about. If any danger lurked for her down here, it was him. Still, he'd made the slight gesture of friendship, and she needed to stay on his good side, at least until she had this story in the bag. "I guess you can call me Laura."

"See? That wasn't so hard, was it? Now tell me why you went to see Felicia when I specifically remember telling you not to."

"Hmm." She tapped her index finger against her chin in a show of pure sarcasm. "Besides the fact that you're not the boss of me, I wanted to find out more about those photos in your kitchen."

"I see." His shoulders tensed as she watched him beneath her lashes. He seemed fascinated with the toes of his shoes all of a sudden, his attention never leaving them as he spoke. "You really should forget about her. She's nothing but a crazy fan, and I'd rather not add more fuel to that fire by putting her in your documentary."

"Who says it was for my documentary?"

He looked up at her then, his gaze wary. "What else would it be for?"

Dammit. She scrambled fast to cover her blunder. "Maybe I just wanted to get to know you better, see why you're so secretive and reclusive all the time." Her foot brushed against his on the sidewalk before she pulled away fast. "She said you took out a restraining order on her because of photos like the ones in your kitchen."

Mike inhaled sharply before relaxing back against the car and staring up into the starry sky above. "Yeah, I did. Not just over photos though. She kept coming around to all of my company's events, trying to flirt with the security, the vendors. Hell, even the caterers. The last straw was when I found out she was schmoozing my programmers to worm her way into parties. I had no choice. She'd made such a nuisance of herself." He shook his head and looked over at Laura. "You're digging into things you know nothing about."

Their feet brushed again, but this time she didn't pull away. Instead, she faced him, her shoulder inches away from his against the Impala. "So, enlighten me."

Mike faced her as well, narrowing the gap between them. His warm, chocolate-brown gaze flickered to her lips before meeting hers again. "Felicia is dangerous. I don't want you to get hurt."

"I can take care of myself." Without thinking, she brushed a stray curl away from his forehead. Yep. His hair felt as silky as it looked. Her fingertips tingled from the brief contact, and her mouth dried. "But thanks for your concern."

"Any time, Laura." His voice lowered, grew huskier, his breath warm and minty as it ghosted over her cheeks. "Any time."

Before she knew what was happening, his mouth was on hers, his lips velvet-soft and tentative, brushing over hers once, twice, before capturing her mouth in a breath-takingly kiss. As if of their own volition, her hands clutched the material of his hoodie then trailed upward over his chest to twine around his neck, her fingers tangling in the soft curls at the base of his neck.

Careful.

Panicked, Laura pushed him away and stepped back, her breath rasping. "I-I have to go."

"Laura, wait. Please, let's talk about this," he called as she ran around the Impala and pulled open the driver's-side door. "Laura, I—"

"No. This was a mistake." She climbed behind the wheel and jammed the key into the ignition, gunning the engine and pulling away before he had a chance to stop her.

Mistake didn't begin to cover what had happened back there. No matter how badly she wanted him, no matter how much she craved his touch, she couldn't have him. Not until she figured out the truth behind the widow's murder. Because if Mike McQuade was somehow involved, then her cavorting with a suspected murderer would be nothing short of career suicide.

***

MIKE WATCHED the receding glow of Laura's crimson tail-lights, berating himself the entire time for his own stupidity. He was a frigging tech genius, for Christ's sake, yet he couldn't seem to get a handle on his own damned libido.

Yes, she'd looked amazing under the soft yellow halo of the streetlamps.

Hell no, he should never have indulged in that kiss.

As he made his way back around the corner to where his driver waited, he couldn't stop reliving the painful breakups from his past. None of his relationships had ever lasted more than a few months at most, mainly because his girlfriends always complained he kept things from them, kept them at a safe emotional distance, never allowing them to get to know the real him.

They should've been grateful.

The real Mike McQuade was no prize.

Not by any definition.

He thanked the driver for holding the door, then climbed into the quiet interior of the sleek black limo and settled against the cool leather seat. He'd hurt far too many people on his road to success. Burned more bridges and massacred too many of his darlings to ever hope to make restitution.

No. Laura Rockford had definitely made the right choice when she'd run far and fast away from him. Better she find out now, discover exactly what kind of monster he was before either one of them got too involved.

Mike shifted in his seat and stared out the tinted window at the passing scenery, taking a deep breath to calm his still-pounding pulse. He licked his lips and still tasted her there, scrubbed his hand over his face and caught the scent of her lingering on his clothes—sweet floral perfume and warm woman.

Cursing, he clenched his fist against his thigh and closed his eyes.

I can't be weak.

7

———

Late the next morning, Laura sat at her usual table in the corner of the 1020 café, scowling at the front page of the *Chronicle*. She wasn't sure which was worse—that J.J. had handed her story about the widow's murder and the byline over to Thad Davis, another staff reporter and her biggest rival, or that Davis had royally skewed the facts to support his opinion of what had happened.

According to him, Felicia Gomez was the murderer, and the case should be closed.

He'd even coined a cheesy tabloid name for the killing, the "Vintage Vegas Murders".

Laura closed her eyes and took a deep breath.

It could have been worse, she supposed.

He could have fingered Mike for the killings.

Mike.

Ugh.

She covered her face with her hands and cringed. That kiss. God, that kiss. It had been heaven and hell all rolled into one. Mike McQuade was the absolute last man on planet Earth she should be kissing. Not with an ongoing murder investigation in which he was involved —if not the new prime suspect—and the fact she was the reporter on his case.

Or at least she had been. Until this morning.

Dammit. She refused to let J.J. and Davis steal her story. She'd keep working on it without them knowing. Especially after the way Davis had bungled everything. Yes, Felicia seemed to be an obvious choice for the widow's death, but it all just seemed a bit too easy, a bit too cut and dried for Laura's taste. Besides, her instincts told her there was more to this situation. And her instincts were never wrong.

"Hey, Sis."

Laura jumped and looked up to see Liv standing before her little table for two, her grin large and her coffee even larger. "Sorry. Didn't mean to scare you."

"It's fine." Laura gathered her newspaper together and shoved the jumbled mess into her messenger bag on the floor, then pointed to the chair across from her. "Sit."

"What's going on?" Liv slid into the seat with her usual cool grace, her appearance immaculate as always. Well, if you didn't count those few stray white hairs on her sharp black suit. That was odd. Laura squinted, intrigued. Short and coarse, they appeared to be cat or maybe dog. Except her sister didn't own any pets. Too messy, she'd always said.

Laura glanced up and caught Liv watching her, brow raised and expression expectant.

"I'm sorry." She leaned back in her seat as her sister sat forward. "Can you repeat the question?"

"I said something's obviously up with you. We meet here every Wednesday, same time, same table, and you still seemed shocked to see me. Don't make me wrestle it out of you. You know I always win."

"It's nothing." Laura gave a dismissive wave, pulling her own cup of cappuccino closer. "Just distracted."

"Distracted, huh? What's his name?"

"Funny." Thanks to her sister, fresh visions of Mike and their kiss swamped her senses. Heat stormed her cheeks and she shifted in her seat, lowering her gaze. "You see the *Chronicle* this morning?"

"No. I had errands. Haven't even had a chance to sit down until now." Liv hooked her designer purse over the back of the chair. "Why?"

Laura pulled the newspaper from her bag and handed it over. "My editor gave the story I've been investigating on Mike McQuade to Thad Davis."

"Shit." Liv scanned the story then glanced at Laura over the top of the paper. "Want me to go kick his ass for you?"

"Tempting as that sounds, no. It's my own fault for

sending him all my research without a verbal consent he'd let me write it."

"But it's your work. Your research. He can't just pass it off to some dickhead who doesn't write half as well as you do."

Laura gave a small smile. No matter what, her family would always have her back. "He screwed up the details too. The artist he mentions in there, Felicia Gomez? I went and talked to her last night. And yeah, her work eerily resembled that crime scene, but my gut tells me there's more going on. It's all just too neat and tidy, too easy." She snorted. "Not that Davis would know. He's got the journalistic chutzpah of a day-old dog turd."

Liv chuckled. "Descriptive. See? That's what I mean. You are so much better than this guy. Your editor must be a total idiot for not recognizing that."

"I think J.J.'s just too swamped to care at this point. They laid off a bunch of his underlings a few months ago, so he's taken on triple the workload. It's not personal," she sighed. "At least I don't think it is. Just expedient. Besides, like I said, Davis got it all wrong. He made it all about Mike's video game and that artist and left out important details that suggest there are other suspects the police are investigating."

Like Mike, her subconscious supplied helpfully.

Laura pushed it aside. There was no direct evidence pointing to him.

Not yet anyway. Stupid subconscious.

"Mike, huh?" Liv stared at her, far too perceptive for Laura's comfort. "Well, whatever. That should be your name on the byline, not Dog Turd Davis."

This time, Laura laughed too. "Thanks. Now I'll never be able to look at that guy again without having that nickname ringing in my head."

"You're welcome." Liv grinned. "So, tell me what else is wrong."

"Isn't that enough?"

"Sure, but I'm your big sister. I know you, and I can tell when there's trouble brewing. So spill it."

The urge to tell someone about Mike and what had sparked between them on that darkened street corner was nearly overwhelming. The fact she and Liv had always confided in each other about their love lives, both good and bad, didn't help either. But she held back. After all, what was she supposed to say? *Oh, yeah. I kissed a really awesome guy last night, but he might also be a cold-blooded, homicidal maniac?*

"Really, there's nothing else." She steered the conversation in a different direction, hoping to throw Liv off track. "It's just I've worked so hard at that job, trying to get ahead, and then this."

She traced a finger around the rim of her green-and-teal cardboard coffee cup. The rich chocolate color of the liquid inside reminded her of Mike's warm brown gaze. *Stop it. Stop thinking about him. Why can't I stop thinking about him?* "I'd almost consider quitting if I had another job to fall back on."

Liv frowned. "You could always come back to Rockford Security."

"Right. Because journalists and private security go so well together."

"C'mon. You're welcome to come back any time. You know that. Blake would be in seventh heaven to have all of us under his constant scrutiny again."

"Yeah, I'm sure he would." Her oldest brother meant well, but he took his role of eldest son and protector quite seriously. Too seriously for Laura's taste. "Really, though, where would you put me? You're in charge of operations, Garrett does the sales, Logan handles the money, and Blake...well Blake oversees the whole circus. There's nothing for me to do."

"Got the circus part right," Liv chuckled. "But I'm telling you, if you want to come back, I'll find you something. Trust me, there's plenty of work to go around. And you're a stakeholder in the company. You get priority status."

"Priority status, huh? Sounds like a nice way of saying you'll invent a job title for me."

"Maybe we'll start up a corporate espionage department. You could be our in-house cyber spy."

"Great. Remember to set up a special budget line to bail me out of prison once they arrest me too. Hacking is illegal. You know that's illegal, right?"

"Whatever. Like all your 'research' is completely on the up and up." Liv used air quotes for emphasis. "You've got skills, Sis. We'll make good use of them at Rockford."

Okay, sure. Maybe her methods weren't always exactly kosher, but she was very careful and always covered her tracks. And any hacking she did was on the small scale. If Rockford Security decided to go in that direction, they'd need to beef up their IT department bigtime just to handle all the extra workload. Not to mention the fact she loved being a journalist. She'd only mentioned quitting to divert attention.

Seems it had worked too. Maybe too well. Time to turn the tables again. "Tell me about your errands this morning."

"What? Why? Nothing but boring stuff—dry cleaners, grocery, drugstore."

"You're pretty dressed up for running errands. And you've got something." Laura gestured toward the right side of her own chest to indicate the hairs on her sister's otherwise pristine outfit. "Kind of unusual for you."

Liv scowled down at the lapel of her jacket and picked off the offending items. "Must've gotten them in the dry cleaners. There was a woman ahead of me with one of the frou-frou dogs in her purse." She uncrossed her legs, then recrossed them, away from Laura this time, flipping her long brown hair over her shoulder in her perfect shampoo-ad style. Her gaze darted from her coffee to the other patrons to the abstract art on the walls, anywhere but at Laura. "Kind of nosy, aren't you?"

"Kind of." Laura grinned. Liv was hiding something, but she'd let her sister keep her secrets, for now. Made her feel better knowing she wasn't the only one. After several more minutes of companionable silence, she checked her watch and sighed. "Well, I should get going."

"What's on your agenda for today?"

"I've got another fluff piece due for J.J. by the end of the week. The incredible hundred-and-five-year-old woman. Plus, I've got a couple more leads to follow up on."

"Leads? For what?" Liv's green eyes narrowed. "Oh. You're going to keep working this case, aren't you?"

"I need to discover the truth, and Lord knows Davis won't do it." She stood and slung her messenger bag across her body. "Besides, if there is more to it, there's a chance I can still break an even bigger story and save my byline."

"Huh. Well, just be careful, okay?"

"I will." Laura gave Liv a quick kiss on the cheek then headed toward the door. "Call you later."

"You better," Liv called back, waving.

Laura headed out to her Impala, climbed into the car and tossed her bag onto the passenger seat before starting the engine. Her day hadn't started well, but if her upcoming appointment proved fruitful, she just might get her huge scoop yet.

Two hours later, Laura parked at the curb in front of a modest-looking, ranch-style home in Henderson, Nevada. She double-checked the address with the one she'd found online then shoved her phone back into her messenger bag and got out.

Showing up at the home of a murder victim unannounced wasn't her usual MO—especially when there were minors involved. But she needed to get the truth about the widow who'd been killed at the El Cortez, for her sake as well as for the sake of the woman's kids. The half-assed article Davis published hadn't even come close.

She walked up the narrow, short sidewalk to the front door and rang the bell, smoothing her hands down the legs of her jeans then running her fingers through her hair. A slight, hot breeze stirred, and she was sure her loose curls were probably a mess by now, but it was too late to do anything about them.

A boy answered. Okay, not really a boy. More like a young man. He looked about eighteen, with spiky dark-blond hair and sad eyes. Laura's heart pinched at the loss of his only living parent. Her family was so close, she couldn't imagine life without her parents around at this point, and she was thirty. Losing both her mom and dad while she was still a teenager was unthinkable.

She swallowed around the sudden lump in her throat and flashed what she hoped was a comforting smile. "Hi. My name's Laura Rockford, and I'm a friend of Mike McQuade's. I was hoping I might be able to speak with you and your sister, if she's available."

The kid looked her up and down, wary. His Marvin the Martian T-shirt clung to his slim torso. "Mike didn't tell me anyone was stopping by."

So Mike had contact with the widow and her family? Seems her gamble had paid off. She faked a wince. "Oh, shoot. He was supposed to call you guys and let you know I'd be coming over, but he was in the middle of a new game design and—"

"Never mind." He opened the door a smidge wider. "That happens a lot."

"What? Him forgetting to call you guys?" Her radar blipped again. She hesitated. "So, it's okay if I come in then?"

"Yeah, I guess." The boy shrugged and stepped aside to open the door all the way. "The place is kind of a mess though, with everything that's happened."

"I'm sure it's fine." She stepped into a tiled foyer and glanced around at the tidy Southwestern-style décor. Other than a few stray papers and empty dishes lying around, it looked fine. Better than her own place, which looked like a nuclear warhead had recently detonated nearby. The kid shuffled from bare foot to bare foot, his toes sticking out from beneath the frayed hem of his jeans, and Laura rushed to cover the awkward silence. "I was, uh, sorry to hear about your mom. Are you and your sister doing okay?"

"It's been hard, with Dad gone too."

Laura's heart squeezed a bit tighter at the sorrow in his voice, and she reached into her messenger bag for the gift she'd purchased in preparation for this meeting. She'd always had a sweet tooth, even more so when she was younger and chocolate was her go-to treat. The bag of assorted caramels had looked particularly good. "I picked these up in town. Thought you guys might like a snack."

"Thanks." He took it from her, his gaze lowered. "Wanna sit down?"

"Sure." She followed him into the living room and took a seat on the end of a large leather sectional sofa. Toss pillows and throws were scattered about haphazardly. A somewhat bedraggled bouquet of roses sat on a side table. The place looked lived in and loved. A few family photos were placed around the room—Barbara Newton and her kids, a few older ones with her husband in there as well. Everyone in the pictures was laughing and joyous, with no idea of the tragedy that would befall them in the years ahead. "Is your sister here too?"

"Maggie, there's somebody here to see us," he called before slumping into a matching armchair across from

Laura. He had the lanky, lean lines of a guy who hadn't quite grown into his body yet, his hands and feet too large for his slim frame. She glanced at the textbook and papers on the coffee table and spotted his name. Geoff. His voice still held a note of suspicion, his dark eyes narrow. "You Mike's new girlfriend?"

Images of their kiss bombarded her brain once more before she clamped a lid on them. Laura tucked a wayward curl behind her ear and looked away. "Just friends."

A petite girl with shoulder-length light-brown hair—straight and held back with a pink headband—walked in, her cautious stare lingering on Laura before darting to her brother. She looked about a foot shorter than Geoff and was dressed in trendy fuchsia sweats. "Who's she?"

"Her name's Laura. She's a friend of Mike's."

"Oh." Maggie propped a hip on the arm of the chair next to her brother and looked Laura up and down. Her single-syllable response sounded both surprised and cynical. Quite a feat for someone who couldn't have been more than sixteen. The girl kind of reminded Laura of herself at that age. "Did Mike send you?"

"He asked me to check in on you guys and make sure you're doing okay." She glanced around again and spotted an open kitchen near the back of the space— newer stainless steel appliances, oak cabinets, granite countertops. "You guys have food? Do you need anything?"

"We're not idiots." Geoff gave her an exasperated glare. "And our aunt is staying here with us too. She handles all the cooking and shopping and stuff."

"Oh, okay. That's good." Laura took off her messenger bag and set it on the sofa next to her, collecting her thoughts. "Have the police found out anything else about what happened to your mom?"

"Not yet." Maggie said. "We told them she'd been acting weird lately though."

"Weird how?"

"It's probably just because the anniversary's coming up."

"Anniversary?"

"Of when Dad died. Five years ago," Geoff said.

"Oh." Laura frowned, her chest constricting. The casual response belied the shadow of pain crossing his boyish features. "I can't imagine how hard this must be for you both."

"We're dealing," he said with a shrug. The kid was cute in the current boy-band style that seemed to drive all Laura's young preteen cousins crazy. Geoff glanced up at his sister. "Right, Maggie?"

She lifted one shoulder, a small frown creasing the area between her dark brows. "What about that creeper? You tell her about that?"

"Creeper?" Laura's ears perked. She reached into her

bag and pulled out her small pad and a pen as discreetly as possible. "Someone's been lurking around here? Did you tell the cops?"

"I'm sure it's nothing, but yeah, I told them. Mags and I saw some guy outside a couple times while we were waiting for the bus last week. Mom said she would handle it. Then..."

Then she died.

The words hung heavy in the air, unspoken.

Laura jotted a few notes on her pad, hating to cause the kids more pain but knowing she had to get to the truth. For them and for herself. "Did she talk to this guy?"

"Not sure. All I know is she made us go over to our aunt's house while she was gone." He shifted in his seat. "When she came back to get us, she seemed calmer though. So maybe."

"Do you know where she went? While you guys were at your aunt's?"

"No." Maggie said, her cheeks coloring. "Sometimes she went to see Mike. I think they were—"

"Shut up, Mags." Geoff gave his sister a warning stare.

Laura blinked hard and stared at her hands in her lap. Had Mike been sleeping with the murdered widow? Her heart sank. She didn't want to believe it, but the kids made it sound like there was more than friendship between their mom and Mike. "So, you think Mike and your mom might've been dating?"

"Maybe." Geoff toyed with the hem of his shirt. "She went to see him every month since Dad died. He gives her money."

"Money?" She did her best to keep her tone even. "For what?"

"Don't know." Geoff's expression said the exact opposite. He might not say it, but it was obvious he thought his mother and Mike were lovers. "All I know is she'd go over to see him every month, and afterward, we had new money in our bank accounts. But that's the only reason I can afford to go away to college next year, so I'm not complaining." He scrunched his nose and sniffed. "At least that was the plan, you know. Before..."

Before their lives went haywire.

Laura pinched the bridge of her nose between her thumb and forefinger. This was harder than she'd anticipated. Interviews with the grieving were always tough, even more so when they involved minors. But these kids seemed so isolated and sad. No matter how much money Mike might've thrown their way, it would never be able to erase the loss of both their parents.

Sudden indignation flared hot in her chest. Why had Mike tossed cash their way? Guilt? Remorse over having an affair with their mother behind their dad's back and then their dad dying unexpectedly? "Does Mike come around here a lot?"

"No. Not really. Not anymore," Maggie said, her foot

tapping against the side of the chair as if to expel some excess energy. "He's been really good to us though. He even sent over a bunch of food and supplies as soon as we heard the news about Mom. And he paid for all of her expenses. You know, for the funeral and...stuff."

Conflicted, Laura pushed to her feet and picked up her bag as the room seemed to press in around her. She needed to get out of this claustrophobic environment and get some fresh air. Part of her wanted to hug Mike for taking these newly minted orphans under his wing. The other part of her couldn't help searching for other motives behind his generosity.

He'd never once mentioned he knew Barbara Newton or her family during their interview, and if he had been sleeping with her prior to her death, then that would certainly be a good excuse as to why he'd kept silent on the subject. After all, nothing screamed motive more than sleeping with the victim. That would also explain his donations to the kids' college funds. Perhaps he was trying to pay his way to a clear conscience.

Definitely lots of new angles to consider.

"Uh, thanks for talking to me, kids." She gave them both a brief smile then rushed for the front door. "I've got to get back to the office. Will your aunt be home soon?"

"She gets off work at five." Geoff trailed after her into the foyer. "Thanks for the candy."

"You're welcome." Laura hurried out into the late-afternoon heat. She didn't breathe again until she was back in the Impala with the air conditioning blasting in to her face. Whatever she'd been expecting to discover in that house, it hadn't been that Mike was romantically involved with the victim or that he was financially supporting her kids.

She closed her eyes and leaned back against the seat.

Seemed the deeper she dug in this case, the less she knew. Still, no matter what the hell was going on with this twisted tale, she was too far in now to ever back out. She had to see this through to the end. Even if that meant discovering Mike was the killer.

8

———

Early the next morning, Laura switched on the police scanner in the Impala during her drive in to the *Chronicle* offices just outside town. Maybe she'd catch a lead on another new story, something that didn't involve gruesome murder scenes or vintage video games or a certain sexy-as-hell, enigmatic, infuriatingly reticent tech mogul.

At first there was nothing but static, broken by the occasional smack-talk banter between the officers and the dispatch operators. She'd made it as far as the iconic Welcome to Las Vegas sign near the side of the highway when a new call came in. Laura half listened as she pressed a bit harder on the accelerator, her pulse picking up speed as well—body found, dressed in 1940s-style clothing, near the Mob Museum.

Damn. She'd just been in that area, getting her morning coffee at Café 1020.

Close to breaking a new land speed record, she veered the Impala into a U-turn and headed back toward the reported destination. If she got there before the cops, she might be able to get closer to the victim this time, get better footage, discover more clues. It was too early to know if it was related to the earlier murder, but how many people could there be running around dressed like old-time gangsters?

Even in Vegas there were limits to the weirdness.

Once she reached the general vicinity, to be on the safe side she parked one street over and took the back way to the museum to avoid running into any of the guys from the station. The radio call had mentioned the body was discovered near the old mailboxes toward the back of the place. If she wasn't mistaken, there was a side entrance close to that spot. Perfect.

Laura pressed her back against an adjacent building and peeked her head around the corner, scanning the area. Red and blue lights flashed from the other end of the short alleyway, and her hopes for arriving before the police faded. They were on the ball today. Yellow crime scene tape had already been strung around the side entrance where she was headed, but there didn't appear to be anyone guarding the propped-open door. Bless their little blue-blood hearts. She smiled. Plus, it would save her from a breaking-and-entering charge if she got caught.

Sticking to the shadows, she crept over, slipped beneath the tape, and entered the building. As she tiptoed down the brick hallway, she peeked into several rooms to make sure no one was around. She'd been in here a couple of times since the place opened back in 2012. The bar still looked the same, with its curved velvet banquettes and pictures of deceased gangsters covering the walls. The next room held the Wall of Infamy, Al Capone's grinning face sneering back at her from the wall as if he approved of her sneaky activities.

Finally, she reached the rows of small original mailboxes set into the walls that were left over from when the place used to be the old post office and courthouse. Several floodlights had been set up around the cordoned off space, casting a harsh glow on the macabre scene.

On the floor, slouched against the wall, was the victim. This time, the killer had used a gun, the blood from the bullet wound to the victim's head smeared down the wall as he'd fallen. The unfortunate guy looked young —maybe mid-twenties, she guessed—clean shaven and unobtrusive looking. He'd been dressed in a white dress shirt and brown waistcoat with matching suit trousers. A newsboy cap sat at a jaunty angle on his head, and black-and-white oxford shoes covered his feet. Hell, from what Laura could see, he'd fit right in on the set of *Newsies*.

With one hand, she fumbled in the pocket of her messenger bag for her phone. She wanted to get video of this one too, for comparison. She'd had her doubts at first, but after seeing this guy, it was pretty obvious these murders were related. And if she remembered right, this was level four in Mike's game. She'd kept playing that too, strictly for research purposes, of course. She'd gotten pretty good too, moving up from a lowly mob runner to a crime boss in less than a week. Not bad. Laura pulled out her device and tapped the screen to bring up her camera.

"You shouldn't be here."

She jumped and turned fast. Troy.

Damn.

"This is for my story." She gave him a coy smile. "I just need a bit of footage so I can connect the dots."

"Dots, huh?" He stepped under the tape and moved in beside her. "Explain."

"Seriously?" She gestured toward the body. "Look at him. The old-fashioned clothes, the pose from the game, the—"

"Game?" He scowled. "What game?"

"Oh." She aimed her phone toward the body and pressed Record. Apparently Troy didn't know about *Vegas Noir* yet. And if the police hadn't made the connection, she wasn't about to do their work for them. This was her best lead yet. "Did I say game? I meant lame. The lame pose."

"Right." He crossed his arms and raised a brow. "Because you always have a hard time saying exactly what you mean." Troy shook his head slowly. "You know something, don't you, Laura?"

"No." She took a panoramic shot of the whole scene then clicked off her phone and slid it back into her bag. "Well, nothing for sure yet. It's just a hunch."

"A hunch, huh?" One corner of his full upper lip quirked up, Elvis style. "You realize not disclosing pertinent information to a law enforcement officer is tantamount to impeding a murder investigation. I could throw you in jail. Then again, maybe you'd like that. Might give you more time to think about your 'hunch.' I've already got you for trespassing on a crime scene."

As if to reinforce his point, Troy removed his handcuffs from his waistband and dangled them in front of her face. He'd do it too, she was sure, if for no other reason than having her at his mercy.

"Fine." She exhaled. Davis's crappy article had pretty much ensured the game's involvement wasn't much of a secret anymore anyway. "*Vegas Noir*. A local tech guy designed the game and made a boatload of money off of it. This scene and the one the other day at the El Cortez are both staged to look like levels from that game. Right down to the victims' clothing and the locations of the kills. They've got to be connected."

"Yeah, I saw the *Chronicle* piece this morning." Troy lowered the handcuffs and stepped closer. "Is that why you're here, Laura? Researching the next big story? And I thought you just wanted to see me again." The stark early-morning sunshine shadowed his classically handsome features, his cocky smile, his teeth even and white against his tanned skin. "I'm far more interesting than some geeky gamer, Laura. Bank on it."

Laura swallowed hard but refused to back down. The fact he looked like some beefcake underwear model should've made her weak at the knees. After all, he was the type she'd always dated in the past—strong, chiseled, self-involved enough that he posed no threat to her career goals or her heart. Hell, until a few days ago, she'd even considered dating him. Then she'd ended up in the arms of a particular video game guru who now seemed to be the only man she wanted.

Not that that was any of Troy Atkins's business.

"This has nothing to do with Mike McQuade." The words emerged with less conviction than she hoped. "It's my job."

Troy's blue gaze narrowed and dropped to her lips before meeting her eyes again. "I hope for your sake that's true, Laura. He's dangerous. And he's a suspect. Stay away from him. Let this drop, or I may not have a choice next time about bringing you in. Understand?"

Ultimatums had never been her forte. Especially ones issued by men who had their own agendas where she was concerned. And since when did the police have Mike listed as a suspect? Had they found out about the money he'd paid Barbara and the kids? She doubted it, but still they must have something if they'd added him to the list of possible murderers.

"Listen, Laura. You're my friend, and hopefully someday maybe more. I don't want our relationship to be like this." Troy gently led her out of the crime scene area. "How about we go to dinner tonight and forget about all this stuff for awhile?"

Dinner with him was the last thing on her mind, but perhaps it would give her a chance to find out more about what they had on Mike and this new victim. Dinner seemed too committed though, too much like a date. "Make it lunch instead and you have a deal."

"Lunch it is. Today. One-thirty work for you?"

"Works for me." She smiled, relieved to be off the hook. "You got my number?"

"Always. See you around, Rockford."

"See ya," she said, backing away toward the corner of the other building.

"Hey," Troy called out from behind her.

"Yeah?"

"Call me if you come across any new information, okay?"

"Will do." Laura gave him a thumbs-up. "You'll be the first person I call."

"HAVE YOU PLAYED THIS YOURSELF YET?" Mike looked up from the pages of computer coding and technical description and over at Ted. The guy's work had improved tremendously since the last time he'd checked in.

Ted relaxed back against the overstuffed cushions of the sofa in his penthouse. Mike noticed Ted seemed more confident today. He'd done excellent work on this code and Mike wondered if that was boosting his self esteem. Whatever it was, Mike was glad to see him just a tad more outgoing. Employees who spoke in more than single-syllable grunts and without moody tantrums were so much easier to deal with.

Ted squared his thin shoulders and held Mike's gaze for longer than his usual two seconds. "Of course. I've tested all the levels, and they're all working great."

"Good. We'll still have to test it on the various gaming platforms to make sure the combinations require an equal level of skill all around, but overall I like the improvements."

"What about the changes to the animation?" His tone held an undercurrent of eagerness that made Mike smile. "I think it's a lot more realistic and lifelike."

Mike grinned. Ted reminded him of himself when he'd first started out. Seemed every sentence the guy uttered ended with his voice rising slightly, making every statement sound like a question.

He tempered his criticism with praise. After all, the

last thing he needed right now was Ted relapsing back into his old ways, where any negative comments about his work resulted in him looking more like a kicked puppy than one of the top game engineers in the industry. "The animation's good. A bit choppy in some places, but I'm sure we can smooth it out in postproduction. The basic concept is super good though. My only suggestion is a bigger flourish near the end of the combo, something to distinguish it from just another series of moves."

Ted sat forward and nodded. "So maybe like a time allocation slider? How about three different ones for three different levels? One that gives different story options, one that gives different dialogue options, and maybe one that gives boosted energy XP?"

"Yeah. Exactly." Mike's smile widened. The fact Ted was brainstorming and giving ready input reminded him of their early days together, before *Vegas Noir* hit it big and reminded him again of why he'd hired the guy in the first place. Quirky or not, Ted was brilliant. "I love it. Let's roll with the idea, and we'll sit down again when you come up with a final plan."

The security buzzer rang, and Mike excused himself. The small flat screen near his keypad in the foyer flashed on, showing the lobby camera feed.

Laura Rockford appeared, all sexy smile and forbidden fruit.

Shit.

At the sight of her, his pulse thudded hard in his

chest, and his whole body tingled. That kiss the other night had made him half crazy, but he refused to acknowledge that it might be anything more than a strong, brief attraction. *But damn, that kiss though.*

He rubbed a hand over his face and pressed the Talk button. "Yes?"

The word emerged rougher than he'd intended.

"Can I come up?" She held up two coffees from the 1020 Café. "Just for a few minutes."

Warmth spread through his system. She remembered his favorite drink. The fierceness with which he wanted to see her again made him take a step back and a deep breath. Seeing her again was a bad idea for both of them, yet he couldn't seem to stop himself from punching in the code that would bring the elevator up to the penthouse.

Nearly vibrating with nervous energy, he waited for the doors to open. Would things be awkward after the other night? Should he grab his hoodie, his virtual armor, to keep him from feeling so vulnerable, so exposed? Could he keep his cool when his blood bubbled with anticipation whenever she was in his vicinity?

The elevator dinged and Laura stepped off, her smile vague and her expression unreadable. If she felt any residual feelings for him after their kiss, she didn't show it.

Mike cleared his throat and struggled to keep his

demeanor impassive. Two could play the pretend game. Hell, he was an expert at pretending these days. "What brings you by?"

"I'm not done with my documentary and have a few more questions, if that's okay."

She was still maintaining her filmmaker ruse, and that lie helped cool his ardor a bit. Thankfully. Mike glanced into the living room where Ted sat scribbling notes on his game. "Um, now's not really ideal. I've got meetings. Can we maybe do lunch later?"

"Oh." Her pretty hazel gaze flicked away from his. "Lunch won't work for me. I've got a date."

Date? He quickly covered his frown by biting his lips. His male ego bristled. Laura certainly hadn't kissed him like she was dating anyone else. Who was this guy? Maybe she was lying.

"Fine." Mike raked a hand through his hair and sighed. "But we'll have to make it fast."

***

"No problem." Laura followed Mike into the kitchen and set the coffees on the center island. He wasted no time in grabbing his and taking a large gulp, she noted, chuckling. Maybe he'd only let her come up for the caffeine, but she intended to make the most of the opportunity. "Did I get your order right?"

"You did," he said after he'd swallowed, grinning at

her over the top of his coffee cup. Her heart did a little somersault. "Thanks for remembering."

"No problem."

"Hey, I'm going to head back to the office to input some of this new coding." Ted said from the doorway. He shrugged into his jacket and gave Laura a hesitant little wave. "Hi, again."

"Hi. Sorry, I didn't know you would be here, or I would have brought a coffee for you too." Laura realized they'd never actually been formally introduced and she extended her hand. "I'm Laura Rockford."

Ted's handshake was somewhat limp and dull. Kind of like his personality, Laura thought.

"Nice to meet you." Ted cracked a half smile that looked like it might have hurt his face and left.

Laura turned back to face Mike, an awkward silence falling. They both gazed around the spacious kitchen, looking at anything but each other. At last, her attention caught on another green-and-teal cardboard cup resting near the top of his trash can. "Looks like you made your coffee run to 1020 again this morning too."

"Of course."

"Did you see the new murder scene?"

"No." He lowered his coffee slowly, his expression surprised. "What happened?"

"The police received an anonymous call around five-thirty. Body found at the Mob Museum. I stopped by the scene on my way in to the office, and it was just like the widow, except a guy this time. Dressed and posed just like in your game."

"Wow." He set his cup back on the island, his movements smooth despite the slight note of tension in his voice. "That's freaky."

"Yeah." She studied his posture—arms crossed, toe tapping against the tile floor—he appeared calm, but there was excess energy simmering beneath his cool surface. He was definitely hiding something. Now she just needed to figure out what. Her mind went back to what Barbara Newton's kids had said. Clearly Mike knew them better than he was letting on, but he owed her no explanation for his past friendships or lovers. Not if they were innocent relationships. She certainly didn't expect him to list off all the women he'd dated. But Barbara had been more than that. He'd paid for the funeral and had sent money to her kids. "I'm surprised you didn't see anything. The whole place was crawling with cops."

"Cops in Vegas aren't that unusual. Plus, I was probably on the phone, so my attention was diverted." He straightened and checked his watch. "Listen, if you have questions, we better get started. I've got a conference call in a half hour."

"Oh, sure. And I'm meeting someone at one-thirty for lunch."

He gave her a quizzical stare, then gestured for her to follow him into the now-deserted living room. Laura took her usual seat on the sofa while Mike sat in the chair across from her. Same as before, except now every time she glanced at him, all she could think about was the brush of his lips against hers.

Crap.

She tucked a strand of hair behind her ear, reminded herself that he was a suspect at least in her eyes, and pulled out her notebook, hoping to get her errant thoughts back on track. "How do these murders make you feel?"

"Excuse me?"

"You never mentioned you knew the first victim, Barbara Newton."

He rested his elbows on the arms of the chair and steepled his fingers, tapping his index fingers against his lips, his gaze narrowed. "Do you have any idea how much I hate this?"

"Hate what?"

"Having my privacy invaded."

Laura resisted the urge to squirm under his scrutiny. "It's the price you pay for fame in our society, unfortunately."

"But I never asked to be famous. All I ever wanted was to create my games. That's it."

"And those games have made you a rich man." She clicked her pen then met his gaze. "Wealth brings an entirely different set of issues."

"Tell me about it." He looked away, toward the stunning view of Vegas out his floor-to-ceiling windows. "Did you know the tabloids have started calling these the Vintage Vegas Murders?" He snorted, the sound harsh and unpleasant. "Hell, the guy at the *Chronicle* all but named me as the culprit before moving on to blame Felicia. Definitely not the legacy I wanted to leave."

She took a deep breath and asked the question she dreaded, not sure if the answer was something she wanted to hear. "Is that why you're paying for a college education for both of Barbara Newton's kids? Your legacy?"

If her bombshell question jarred him in any way, he didn't show it.

"My reasons are my own," he said, rubbing his thumb over his full bottom lip.

Her sharply honed reporter's instinct told her that, while he was avoiding the question, it wasn't because he was guilty of something as serious as murder. For some bizarre reason, his avoidance only drew her closer, only made her more curious to learn all of his secrets. She straightened, before she embarrassed herself and him. Mike McQuade had obviously moved past their late-night indiscretion, and so should she.

He continued to watch her. "Mind telling me how you found out about that?"

"I happened to meet her son and daughter the other day."

"Oh, really? You just happen to meet with teenagers on a regular basis?"

"Filmmaking takes you into all kinds of situations." Good thing she was used to thinking on her feet. He was clever. Far too clever for her own good. She continued on the same path, different angle. "So, how did you and Barbara Newton know each other?"

Mike grinned, all sexy charm and mystery. "You met with the kids, yet you didn't get the answer to that question, huh? Wonders never cease." He glanced at his watch again. "Sorry, but I'm out of time."

Laura bit her lip in frustration and did her best not to notice the way his eyes followed the small move. "Yes. Right. Fine. Thanks for working me into your busy schedule."

"Sure." He rose and escorted her to the door, his attitude pure professionalism, no hint whatsoever of the man who'd kissed her in front of God and anyone else who'd happened by. "Good to see you again, Laura."

"Yeah, uh, thanks again for letting me come up."

"My pleasure." Mike leaned against the wall near the elevator, repeating the same words he'd said after their very first meeting, the smile on his face not quite reaching his eyes. That look left her unsettled. "See you around, Laura Rockford."

"See you, Mike." The elevator doors slid closed, and she slumped against the wall as the car descended. She'd had almost the identical exchange just hours earlier with Troy, but to very different effect. With Detective Atkins, it was all a game, all good fun to get what she needed.

With Mike, it was a game too—a dark, dangerous, decidedly wicked game of cat and mouse. Unfortunately, she had no idea who was the predator and who was the prey.

The doors opened again, and she walked out into the airy lobby once more.

Lunch with Troy wasn't how she wanted to spend her afternoon, but maybe she could at least find out more about the victim from earlier. Lord knows she'd gotten nowhere with Mike.

In fact, he seemed to foil every attempt she made to get closer to him, a feat that both impressed and infuriated her. Still, as she headed back out to her car, she couldn't help but laugh.

Mike McQuade might be a royal pain in her ass, but he was also intriguing as hell. Life with him would be anything but boring, that was for sure.

Brains and brawn. A lethal combination where her heart was concerned.

9

After Laura left, Mike grabbed his laptop and searched for the latest news on that morning's murder investigation. One killing influenced by his game was a tragedy. Two killings sent a definite message. And yeah, the publicity and the notoriety were gold—sales of *Vegas Noir* had doubled in just the last week alone.

But the continued scrutiny on his private life? Not so much.

The *Chronicle*'s website was the first he checked, but he found nothing new. Laura's probing questions, however, suggested she had more information. Which meant his little reporter had sources within the police department. Mike smiled. Smart girl. Always resourceful. She was like a cat that always seemed to land on her feet, a quirk that kept him both fascinated and wary.

He wondered how long she'd keep up her documentary filmmaker ruse. Longer than he was able to keep his own truths hidden? Either way, his nerves zinged with anticipation.

The security buzzer screeched loudly again in the quiet penthouse, and Mike scowled. He wasn't expecting anyone else today. With a sigh, he set his laptop aside then walked over to the small screen. The faces of the same two detectives who'd interviewed him a few days earlier appeared. Great. Local law enforcement had proved slow in their investigation but not stupid. Not yet anyway. "Yes?"

"Mr. McQuade, Detectives Hopkins and Ruiz from LVPD. We have a few more questions we'd like to ask you. May we come up?"

Refusing would only make them more suspicious, so Mike acquiesced. He waited until they boarded the elevator then typed in the code to bring them to the top floor. Seconds later, a ding chirped and the doors opened. Both men gazed around his place, eyes wide and expressions appreciative. He'd bought the place to impress. Good thing he was getting his money's worth.

Mike led them into the living room and offered them drinks then took a seat across from them when they declined. "How can I help you gentlemen today?"

"Where were you at two a.m. this morning, Mr. McQuade?"

"Uh." He frowned. "Here. In bed. Sleeping."

"Alone?"

"Yes." Mike leaned back in his seat as the cop sat forward.

"How well did you know Ben Sanders?"

He'd not asked *if* he knew Ben Sanders but how well. They'd obviously done their homework. "Was Mr. Sanders the victim?"

"Yep," Hopkins, the bulkier of the two detectives, said. "And you knew the first victim as well. So, tell us about Ben."

With a sigh, Mike sat forward again, ignoring the unease trickling through his blood. "There's not much to tell, honestly. I didn't know him. He worked for one of the catering companies we used for a holiday party a while back. I might have said hello to him in passing a few times. That's all I have to tell. Am I a suspect?"

"The killer dressed him in vintage clothes and staged the scene like another level from your game, *Vegas Noir*. This makes two victims with the same MO. That could signal a serial situation."

Hopkins hadn't answered his question, not really. "I still don't see how this relates to me. Millions of copies of that game have sold all over the world. It's one of the top ten RPGs played of all time. Anyone could've gone off the deep end with it. Not my fault, and hardly grounds to make me a suspect."

The detectives exchanged a look that Mike didn't miss.

"Right." Ruiz spoke up this time. "Well, can you explain why you didn't mention the incident with the first victim's husband during our first conversation?"

"I didn't think it was relevant." Mike gave them a pointed stare. "Is it?"

"Maybe." Ruiz shrugged. "There was an investigation into those circumstances too, correct?"

"Yes, but his death was ruled an accident." He rubbed a hand over his face and struggled to relax his tense shoulders. "Have you found something to suggest otherwise?"

"Not necessarily." Hopkins flipped the small notepad in his hand shut then stood. Ruiz did the same. "Seems strange, though, that both partners in that marriage died so violently."

"Yeah, it's unfortunate." Mike pushed to his feet and followed the cops back out into the foyer. "But—"

"Unfortunate." Ruiz snorted. "That's one way to put it."

Hopkins pushed the button, and the elevator doors slid open once more. Mike stood several feet back and watched them, arms crossed. He hated being defensive, but he couldn't help it. Their questions had struck far too close to home. "We'll be in touch, Mr. McQuade."

"You never did answer me. Am I a suspect?" The

words physically hurt him to say, but he needed to know so he could act appropriately. "Do I need an attorney?"

"Not yet." Ruiz gave him a chilly little smile. "We'll be in touch."

Pulse racing, Mike stood his ground until the doors closed then rushed back to open his laptop once more. This time he typed in the name of victim number two, Ben Sanders. The personal record search listed facts he already knew—twenty-four, part-time college student, full-time waiter for Fantastic Functions Catering. They worked all of M Cubed Gaming's parties. He'd told the cops the truth. The party gig really was his only concrete tie to the victim. Still, it was one tie too many for Mike's comfort. He liked to keep things neat and clean and simple.

The kid's picture mocked him from the screen. Ben had been just starting out in life and had his whole future ahead of him. God, what a waste. And the cops had made the connection to Barbara's husband sooner than he'd expected too.

Dammit.

Mike sat back and stared at the ceiling.

There was another possible tie, one that hadn't occurred to him until now.

Felicia.

Mike had gotten that restraining order because her tactics to get closer to him had taken a decided turn toward crazy. The constant emails and phone calls and stalking had been bad enough. But when she'd switched to harassing his staff in order to gain access to his life, that's where he drew the line. She'd even gone so far as to flirt with the catering staff at his last big event to try and sneak into the party.

Had Sanders been one of those flirtations?

Determined to find out, he stalked into his bedroom and pulled a new disposable phone from his well-stocked cabinet. After setting it up with a fake ID, he called in a quick, anonymous tip to the automated police department hotline indicating they should question Felicia Gomez in regard to Sanders's death.

Then he crushed the device beneath his booted foot and tossed the remains in the trash before stepping out onto the balcony of the penthouse, hoping some fresh air might chase away his lingering doubts. He used to come out here all the time when he'd first moved here, loving the freedom. Now, after what had happened…

No. Mike shook off the brutal memories and stared into the blue expanse of the sky. He'd done his good deed for the day by calling in the tip, though he doubted it would be enough to remove the black marks on this soul. In fact, as the dry desert wind smacked him in the face, he doubted there were enough good deeds in the universe to erase them all.

Pacing back into his penthouse, he stared at the door the police had so recently exited through. The way Ruiz had said they'd be in touch scared the crap out of him. The last thing he needed was the cops taking an interest in him and digging deeper. Because if they found out what had happened in his past, it would not bode well for his future.

10

"So, a new murder investigation, huh?" Not exactly subtle, but Laura had put off asking for info as long as she could. She snuck a side glance at Troy and saw him shake his head, his expression incredulous.

"Seriously? I just bought you the best Cadillac burger in Vegas and all you want to talk about is the dead guy?" He bumped shoulders with her. "Not much for building a guy's ego, are you?"

"What? I said the food was good." She grinned. "Okay. It was really, really good. And thank you." They stopped at the corner a block from her apartment and waited for the light to change. Laura did her best not to fidget. She liked Troy. She did. He was nice, smart, had a good job and all his hair and teeth. A major step up from her recent adventures in dating land. But there was something missing. Not with him, with her. They laughed and talked and had a great time at lunch. But for her, at least, there'd been no spark, no chemistry. Not like there had been with Mike. "What was the guy's name?"

Troy sighed. "You just don't give up, do you?"

"Not unless I'm forced."

He leaned in like he was going to kiss her and she took a step away. He met her gaze and his friendly smile slowly faded. "Ben Sanders. Is that the only reason you agreed to come with me today?"

The blunt question threw her off balance for a second. *Yes.* "No."

"I see." A tiny muscle twitched near the corner of Troy's blue eyes, and she got the distinct impression that he saw directly through her bullshit. "I, uh, should actually get back to the station."

"Don't you want to come up for a sec?"

"Nah." He backed away, hands in his pockets. "Got tons of paperwork to get through."

"Oh. All right." The light turned green and tourists jostled around them. Laura bit her lower lip, remorse flooding her system. Troy was a fabulous guy, just not *her* fabulous guy. She'd not meant to hurt him. "Well, okay then. Guess I'll see you later."

"Yeah." He exhaled. "See you later."

Laura continued to her apartment alone, eager to put the awkward scene with Troy behind her and dig into researching the newest victim. Only problem was when she opened her door, she wasn't alone.

"Do you ever clean around here?" Liv asked, holding a pair of crumpled socks in one hand and a dirty plate in the other. "I swear these were in the exact same spot the last time I came over."

Great. Just what she needed to top off her afternoon of regrets—the Queen of Tidy. Her frustration came out as snark. "Do you ever call before arriving?"

"I'm family. No call required." Liv cleared two seats on the sofa then took one and patted the other. "Now come over here so we can talk."

"Talk?" Laura shrugged out of her coat and tossed it over the back of the nearest chair before taking her place beside her sister. "How long have you been here?"

"Long enough." She smoothed a hand down her perfectly pressed houndstooth trousers then straightened her matching blazer. "I saw you coming down the street. Who's the new hottie?"

"He's not a hottie." Liv raised an incredulous brow, and Laura relented. "Okay, fine, maybe he is a hottie, but he's just a friend. He works for the police department."

"Friend, huh? Wish I could find me some friends like that."

Laura nudged her with her elbow. "Seriously. Troy's a detective with the homicide division. He helps me out with information for my stories sometimes."

"Right. So that's what they're calling it these days?" Liv snickered.

"Shut up. There's honestly nothing between us. At least for me. No spark. Not like…"

"Like?"

"Nobody." She fiddled with the edge of the cushion. When Liv remained silent, Laura finally glanced over to find her sister waiting patiently. Her family always did know the right buttons to push, dammit. "Fine. Mike McQuade, okay? We *might* have kissed the other night, and I *might* have enjoyed it. Way more than I should, actually."

"Wait a minute." Liv's smile morphed into a frown. "You're telling me you're attracted to a guy who may or may not be a murderer. That'll go over well at the next family dinner."

"I know." Laura tossed up her hands, exasperated. "It's so wrong, I can't even fathom where to begin or why it happened. All I know is that it felt so right. Like everything just clicked between us, you know?"

"Blake is not going to be happy when he finds out."

"Oh, God." Laura groaned. "Please promise you won't say anything to him. I mean, there's no concrete proof Mike's even involved in any of this mess. I mean, whoever's doing it is using his game in their sick backdrops, but that doesn't prove anything, right?" She covered her face with her hands, knowing how lame her arguments sounded. "God, I don't even know *what* I mean anymore.

This is *so* totally not like me. Not at all. But I can't seem to help myself when he's around."

"What do your instincts tell you about him?"

Laura rested her head against the back of the sofa. "That he didn't do it. That he's innocent."

"Got any facts to support that conclusion?"

"A few. There's at least one other viable suspect. The crazy fan Davis mentioned in his article. Felicia Gomez. She's unhinged enough to give her a good motive."

"Ha! Dog Turd Davis to the rescue again." Liv chuckled, and the somber mood in the room lightened. "At least that lying bastard's good for something, right?"

"Right." Laura shook her head. "What am I going to do, Sis?"

"Well, I think you need to get to the bottom of this, one way or another. If Mike is someone you think you want in your life, you better make damned sure he's one of the good guys. Otherwise Blake will skin him alive."

"I can do that."

"Good." Liv pushed to her feet and grabbed her purse. "Now I better go. I stopped to see if you wanted to get a late lunch, but since you already ate, I'll just grab something and take it back to the office with me. I've got a bunch of month-end reports to catch up on anyway."

"Sounds good." She followed Liv to the door. They hugged and Liv gave her a short wave before heading out. "I'll call you."

"No, you won't."

"No, I probably won't." Liv grinned. "See ya."

"See ya."

Laura waited until her sister disappeared into the elevator before closing the door. She returned to the sofa and opened her laptop, typing the name of the second victim into her browser. Telling Liv about Mike had somehow made the whole situation seem more real. She didn't know where this thing with Mike would go. Maybe nowhere. But with the body count rising and each clue more strongly pointing the finger in Mike's direction, it was more crucial than ever for her to dig into the evidence to find the truth. She just hoped that whatever evidence she found would help clear Mike's name ... and not help prove him guilty.

An hour later, Laura walked into the aging Regency Apartments a few blocks from her building. According to what she'd found on the Internet, this was the last known residence of Ben Sanders. The fact he'd lived so close to her made Laura feel slightly unsettled. There was a good chance they'd passed on the street a time or two, maybe even greeted each other. Years as a reporter had given her a tougher skin than most, but still.

This story hit home on far more fronts than she wanted to admit.

She double-checked the address then climbed the

stairs to the fourth floor. The linoleum in the hallway peeled slightly around the edges, and the air smelled musty and stale. Brown water stains clung to the crumbling ceiling tiles, and billowing square exhaust vents blew stray cobwebs in the artificial breeze.

Laura squinted at the gold numbers tacked to the brown painted doors, counting down to the one she wanted—406. She knocked once then checked her watch. Three twenty. Most likely no one home. Perfect. After a glance in both directions, she reached into the pocket of her jacket for the lock picks she always kept on hand for such occasions. She'd just started to pull out the small black leather pouch when the door creaked open.

Her breath caught and her eyes widened.

Felicia Gomez.

The last person she expected to see in this particular location on this particular day was dressed in a man's wrinkled dress shirt, her hair mussed and her eyes red and puffy. She looked like she'd just crawled out of bed. Her voice sounded groggy and rough. "Can I help you?"

"What are you doing here?"

Nose wrinkled, Felicia blinked at her. "I live here. What are you doing here?"

So, Felicia and Ben Sanders were a couple. One more connection between the crazy stalker fan and one less tie between Mike and the murders. Maybe this day would be good for something after all. Still, Felicia seemed awfully unfazed for a woman whose boyfriend had just been killed. Odd. Then again, maybe the police hadn't informed her yet. Laura decided to play cool and see how much she knew. "I, uh, came to see Ben."

A shadow crossed Felicia's pretty features, her stoic expression dissolving into a sorrowful scowl, her voice breaking over the words. "Ben's dead."

"Oh, I—"

The rickety elevators to her right dinged and two men stepped off, Troy and another detective—Hopkins, maybe? Laura couldn't remember the guy's name now. Her gaze darted between the cops and Felicia. Now, at least, she appeared upset enough about her boyfriend's demise, but there were still no tears. Why no tears? Most victims' families cried and wailed in their grief, at least in her experience, but not Felicia. She was either still in shock or a very good actress.

Laura was betting on the latter.

Troy immediately stepped in beside Laura. "What the hell are you doing here?"

The other detective showed his badge to Felicia. "I'm Detective Hopkins, LVPD. Are you Felicia Gomez?"

Felicia nodded, scratching her head and looking completely lost and forlorn. Laura almost felt sorry for her. Almost.

"We have some questions for you, Ms. Gomez," Hopkins said, his tone neutral despite the half-naked woman before him. Laura glanced over at Troy, only to find him staring dutifully at his toes, avoiding Felicia's performance and appearance altogether.

They must teach them that at the academy, she supposed.

Suspect Shunning 101.

"Okay." Felicia stepped aside to open the door wider. "Come in."

"No." Hopkins clasped his hands in front of him. "Down at the station, ma'am. You'll need to get dressed and come with us."

"Am I under arrest?" Felicia seemed to have snapped fully awake at his statement.

"No, ma'am." Troy left Laura's side finally and moved in beside his partner. "Just for questioning. If you resist, however, we can charge you with impeding an ongoing murder investigation."

"Oh." Felicia shuffled her bare feet, frowning. "All right. Let me put on some clothes. You want to come in while I do that?"

"We'll wait in the hall, ma'am." Hopkins stood guard outside the door, and Felicia mumbled something under her breath before closing it.

Troy moved in closer to Laura again. "Answer me."

"What?"

"What the hell are you doing here? This place is dangerous right now. You should go."

"Why? You think Felicia did it?"

The muscles around his tight jaw tensed and he

crossed his arms. "Nope. No more leaks from me today. You reached your quota."

"I thought we were friends, Troy."

"I thought you were going to be more careful, Laura."

Flustered at being caught at her own game, she looked away. "I am careful. Besides, Felicia Gomez is hardly a threat. I could take her blindfolded with one hand tied behind my back."

Troy's blue gaze narrowed. "Who says I'm talking about Felicia Gomez?"

Touché.

Before she could respond, the apartment door opened and Felicia stepped out, dressed now in a pair of faded jeans and an old UNLV sweatshirt. Laura could feel the weight of Troy's stare on her even though she ignored him. As Felicia passed by her, their eyes met, and Laura would've sworn she saw a flicker of guilt cross the other woman's face.

Good. As they all rode down to the lobby together, she couldn't help feeling a bit vindicated. Felicia seemed like the logical choice for murderer. All the pieces fit. Or at least made sense. Either way, it was one less reason to blame Mike for the killings, and that made Laura happy.

Perhaps she hadn't fallen for a diabolical psycho killer after all.

11

***

Laura wandered the streets of Vegas for awhile after leaving the Regency. She could have gone home and tweaked the article she'd started on the second murder victim, added in the new details about Felicia and the police taking her down to the station. Of course, nothing was concrete yet, but everything seemed to point to her now being responsible.

Except she didn't head home.

Instead, she drifted northward, past the 1020 Café and the Mob Museum and the 18b Galleries, all the way to the Turnberry. Damn. She'd not intended to go see Mike, but somehow that's where she ended up.

The same bulky guard that had been stationed at the gate that first day was there again. He gave Laura a little wave as she passed, the fan she'd bought him whirring on the small desk in front of him. This time, though, there was no need for bribery. She'd never gotten around to returning the keycard the concierge had given her that first day, so all she had to do was flash it, and he let her pass without question.

Once inside the lobby, she walked to the elevators, then hesitated. What was she doing here? Mike wasn't expecting her, and she needed to have at least the hint of a credible reason for her unexpected arrival. Something more than not being able to think of anything but him for the past week or the fact she'd walked in a constant haze since their kiss. She supposed she could use the documentary angle again, but she didn't have the camera with her this time. Maybe her phone might make a plausible substitute, given the circumstances.

Satisfied with her story, she pressed the buzzer.

No answer.

Well, crap.

Her shoulders hunched, and disappointment pinched her heart. All because a guy who had no idea she was coming over to begin with wasn't home. Man, she had it bad. This was a stupid idea, anyway. Embarrassingly stupid to be chasing after a guy who she knew nothing about. Except that he was a good kisser.

It was good he wasn't home. To be sure, she pressed the button once more, resolved that if there was no answer this time, she was *so* out of there.

"Yes?" Mike's gruff voice sent a flurry of involuntary shivers down her spine.

She resisted her urge to fidget and instead gave a tiny wave and smile into the camera. "Hey, it's your favorite pest of a filmmaker again. I wondered if you might have a minute for a few final questions."

Silence.

Finally, he sighed. "Okay, but I can only give you twenty minutes."

"Great." She hadn't realized how tightly her hands were clenched until her fingers went numb from lack of blood supply. Laura waited for the doors to ding open then stepped into the elevator. As she rode skyward, she closed her eyes and took several breaths. She could do this. She could get through twenty minutes with Mike McQuade and keep her hands to herself.

She could. She should. She would.

So what if the guy was now most certainly innocent and most certainly interested and available. They were both adults. Adults didn't tackle other adults to the floor and kiss them senseless.

The car jostled to a halt, and the doors opened to reveal Mike, looking hotter than any man had a right to in his body-hugging faded jeans and tight black T-shirt.

Her pulse thudded loud in her ears, and she licked her lips.

"Uh, we can talk in the living room again," he said, turning away. But not before she'd seen the way his gaze narrowed on her mouth or how his dilated pupils made his eyes darker and sexier than usual. She did her best not to stare as he led her into the other room. "You said you had more questions for me?"

"What?" She forced herself to meet his gaze. "Oh, um, yeah. More questions."

"No camera today?"

"No." She took a seat on the sofa and pulled out her phone. "I walked here from my place and didn't want to lug all that equipment around. I'll just take some footage on my phone, if that's okay, then transfer it over in edits."

"Right. Whatever. Sure." He sat down beside her this time instead of across from her, and the soft skin of his bicep brushed against her shoulder. A swarm of excited butterflies took flight inside her. His knee bumped hers, and he mumbled an apology, but he didn't pull away. "So, what else could you possibly have to ask me, Laura?"

She gripped her phone tighter in one hand and flashed him a hesitant smile. "They just took Felicia in for questioning on the second murder."

"Really?" He rested his arm on the back of the sofa behind her, and she did her best not to snuggle into his side. Funny, but she'd expected more of a reaction from him over the news. Relief, maybe, or at the very least agreement with law enforcement's decision to take her into custody for questioning. The gal had stalked him, after all. He had the restraining order to prove it. The fact he seemed to have little to no reaction at all bothered her a little, but she reasoned it away. Mike was a private guy. He didn't let his emotions show. For all she knew, he could have a major buzz over the news.

Mike shook his head, his firm lips quirking into a half smile. "Huh. Wow. Felicia's always been nuts, but I never thought she'd commit murder."

Laura relaxed back into the overstuffed cushions, enjoying his nearness, the sense of intimacy their close proximity created. "Well, you must've had some concerns since you took out a restraining order on her, right? Judges don't issue those without proof of a threat."

"Yeah. I suppose." He ran his free hand through his already messy hair, and she inched just a bit closer to him, drawn by some invisible cord she couldn't explain.

If he noticed how rapt she was, Mike didn't show it. Just kept rambling on about Felicia. "I mean, she used to hang around my offices, acting all crazy and throwing herself at my programmers."

She wanted to ask if Felicia had thrown herself at him too but didn't.

Instead, she shrugged, which caused his fingers behind her back to brush against her shoulder. He maintained the contact, rubbing small, absent circles over her sensitive skin. She glanced over at him, but he continued to stare at the toes of his black boots, frowning, seemingly lost in thought. Feminine resolve bubbled within her. She wanted him to be as aware of her as she was of him. Emboldened, she reached out and laid her hand near his knee, lowering her voice a smidge so he had to lean closer to hear. "Crazed fans will do anything to get close to their obsession. I've seen it happen."

"Really?" He looked at her then, his grin slow and sexy and seductive as hell. "Make a lot of documentaries about obsessed people, huh?"

Laura swallowed hard. He closed a bit more space between them, watching her with his intent brown gaze. A girl could drown in that warm chocolate depth and die a happy woman. Maybe he wasn't as unaffected by their nearness as she'd thought. She tossed her phone aside, all pretense of an interview gone. "I meet all kinds of interesting people in my work."

"I bet you do."

She tipped her face up to his, and he captured her lips once more. A tiny niggle of warning dinged in the back of her mind. Mike was so closed off, offering her very little opportunity to get to know him. What if this was all a ploy to get her to stop asking questions? But then his arm slipped around her waist, pulling her closer.

Screw caution.

Felicia had been taken in for questioning by the police. Until they released or arrested her, Laura would have no further fodder for her burgeoning article. This moment was entirely hers and she surrendered to it.

An annoying buzz started to her right. At first she

ignored it, lost in the feel of Mike's kiss. So good. So damned good she never wanted to leave this space, this man, this moment.

Buzz, buzz, buzz.

Mike chuckled and lifted his head, a brow raised. "Want to get that?"

"No." She sighed and fumbled beside her for her stupid phone. Onscreen flashed an urgent reminder:

ROCKFORD SECURITY
STAKEHOLDER MEETING
15 MINUTES

"SHIT." She tottered to her feet despite the weakness in her knees. "Sorry. Got to go. Work meeting."

"Right." He stood too, not meeting her gaze as he tidied the hem of his T-shirt. "No problem."

With a sigh, she ran a hand through her hair. Considering that she'd now kissed him a second time — and wanted to do it again — now seemed as good a time as any for a dose of truth. Wasn't like she needed to keep her cover now anyway. "I'm, uh, not really a documentary filmmaker. I'm actually a reporter for the *Chronicle*."

"Yeah, I know." He scrubbed a hand over his face. "Thanks for telling me, though."

Confused, she picked up her messenger bag and

swung it over her shoulder. "What do you mean you know?"

"You don't think a man in my position would let just anyone up here for an interview, do you?" He stepped closer and kissed the tip of her nose before walking back out to the foyer. "I knew who you were before we did our first interview."

"Really?" Her passionate haze diminished slightly. "And you just let me go on pretending?"

"Sure." He winked and pressed the elevator button. "After all, you were so cute setting up your camera and all."

"Cute?" Laura wrinkled her nose. "I am not cute."

"How about beautiful, then? Gorgeous? Irresistible?" He punctuated each word with a kiss as she boarded the elevator once more.

"Better." She leaned out for one more kiss then slung her bag over her body and crossed her arms. "Talk to you later."

"Oh, yeah." He grinned, an arm resting on each side of the elevator doors, the position highlighting his physique. As the doors slid closed, he blew her one last kiss. "Bank on it, baby."

The whole ride down to the lobby and the walk back to her apartment passed by in a blur. She'd just made out with Mike McQuade. Laura climbed into the Impala and took stock of her appearance in the rearview mirror.

Pink cheeks, swollen lips, glittering eyes. Yep, she

looked like a woman who'd just been thoroughly kissed and thoroughly enjoyed the experience.

She started the car then pulled out of her spot and headed toward the Rockford Security offices. She needed to get rid of that look and quick. If her family sensed even the slightest hint of romance, they'd pounce on her like mice on Gouda. So at the next red light, she smoothed her mussed hair back into a slick ponytail, made sure all her buttons were done up properly, and dabbed on a fresh coat of lip gloss.

There wasn't much she could do about the flushed cheeks or sparkling eyes, but at least she looked more sedate and normal than before. Blake and Liv were the two she needed to watch out for. With luck, she could just avoid them altogether. She was a bit late arriving, so she'd just stand near the back and escape as soon as the meeting was done.

Easy.

As she pulled into the lot of Rockford Security and climbed out of the Impala, she took a deep breath. Except she'd forgotten one important thing. Where her family was concerned, nothing was ever easy.

Mike stood at the elevator for a long while after Laura left. The last person he should be involved with was Laura Rockford. She'd lied her way into his life and his home, and that alone should have exterminated his trust. Add in the fact she made him feel things he'd thought well out of range for a man like him, and that should have been the final kicker. But try as he might, he couldn't get her out of his system.

He'd thought the first kiss would do it. Then the second. Now this.

Shit. Just shit.

He pressed the heels of his hands into his eyes. What a fucking mess.

Slowly, he walked back into the living room and slumped down onto the sofa, the same spot where moments before he'd held Laura in his arms. Hell, if he put his hand on her cushion, he still felt her heat there. He let his head fall back into the cushions, and the fragrance of her floral perfume wafted around him.

At least she'd finally told him the truth of who she was.

That counted for something, right?

His brain was so scrambled that he didn't know which end was up anymore.

Mike glanced over at his own phone, plugged into its charger on the nearby end table, and spotted an alert on the small screen. He grabbed it and squinted at the message from Ted.

GOT A NEW PROTOTYPE.

THINK YOU'LL DIG IT.

SHAKING HIS HEAD, he clicked off the device and tossed it back onto the table. Ted seemed to have really gotten his shit together lately.

Good.

That made exactly one of them.

12

Laura shifted in her seat at the conference table and did her best to concentrate on Blake droning on and on about facts and figures and every other boring thing under the sun. She loved her oldest brother, loved all her family, but sometimes she'd kill to be an only child. Or at least exiled, like Jace. The guy didn't know how lucky he had it right about now.

She grabbed some veggies from the tray in the middle of the table and did her best to crunch her carrots quietly while Liv—who had somehow ended up in the chair right beside hers despite her efforts to the contrary—continued to pester her about Mike.

"I heard on the radio that they've brought in another person for questioning in that murder case," Liv whispered, glancing at Laura over her shoulder. "Didn't you talk to that artist too?"

"Yeah. Felicia Gomez." She kept her voice low to avoid Blake's detection. "And I was there when the cops took her in earlier."

"Really? Was your cute cop friend there too?"

"The operative word being 'friend.'" Laura gave her sister an exasperated look. "And yeah, Troy was there."

"So no arrest yet?"

"Not yet."

"But this girl is off her nut, right? Sounds pretty guilty to me."

"Guess it's a good thing you're not in charge then, huh? What happened to innocent until proven otherwise?"

"Oh, come on." Liv reached back and smacked her on the arm. "You can't tell me you aren't jumping for joy."

"Why would I care?" She did her best to keep her tone neutral and not let her immense relief show.

"Because it's not *him*."

"Who?"

"Don't play dumb with me, Sis." Liv gave her a disparaging stare. "Mike. Now you two can get down and dirty and keep your conscience clear."

"Something you'd like to share with the rest of us, ladies?" Blake said, his voice stern.

Shit.

Laura felt like she was back in kindergarten getting caught painting some other kid's hair blue because he'd had the gall to say hateful things about her favorite cookie-hoarding monster. "No."

Garrett, her younger brother, snorted. "All I heard was Laura was getting down and dirty with somebody."

"Shut up."

"Bet I know who it is." This from Logan, another brother—older by two years and too nosy for his own good, in Laura's opinion anyway. He grinned at her, his usual arrogant self. "Does his name start with a T?"

"Nope."

Liv chuckled. "His name's Mike McQuade."

"I said, shut up!" She kicked Liv in the shin for good measure. Her love life was none of their business. "I'm not getting down or dirty. With anyone. Drop it."

All eyes remained on her. She wanted to smack the smug looks right off all their faces. Livid, her words to her eldest brother emerged as little more than a growl. "What?"

Blake gave Laura a funny look. "Nothing. If we could get off your love life and get back on track with this meeting, that would be great."

In response, she picked up one of her carrots and hurled it at his head.

He easily ducked out of the way, his mulish expression more appropriate for a spinster schoolmarm than a dashing CEO. "Very mature. Do I need to put you in the corner too?"

"Do it!" Garrett laughed. "I'd pay money to see that."

Laura glared over at him.

"And stop wasting food, Sis." Logan snagged a carrot of his own and swirled it through the bowl of dip in the middle of the tray before shoving it into his mouth. "Mom would be appalled."

She gave him the fakest smile ever and flipped him off for good measure.

"Can we ever have a nice, civilized, normal meeting in this family?" Blake looked ready to string them all up by their toenails. He sighed heavily and picked up his papers again. "Fine. Whatever. Now, for the reason I called this meeting."

Finally. Laura wisely kept that comment to herself.

"I'm sure you all remember Chase Evans." Blake met each person's gaze. When he came to Laura, she nodded. Chase Evans had worked with Blake in a security firm years ago, before Blake founded Rockford Security. Chase had saved Blake's life during an armed robbery attempt, though he'd refused to take any credit for it. None of the Rockfords would ever forget Chase Evans, even though he'd later been convicted on drug-dealing charges. Laura had thought that odd for a guy who worked security and was studying to be a lawyer, but she'd seen odder things. There were extenuating circumstances, if she remembered correctly, not to mention his tough life. Blake continued. "Well, he's about to get out of prison, and I'd like to offer him a job."

Laura shrugged. "Hire him then. You're CEO. You don't need us for that."

"According to our employment guidelines, he's not eligible without board approval," Blake said, "due to his criminal record."

"His 'criminal record.'" Logan added air quotes for emphasis. "Right."

"We all know he took the rap for his brother," Laura said.

"Yeah. Chase is fine." Liv straightened. "Now, if you wanted to hire his brother, I'd have a problem."

"Good." Blake's tense posture relaxed. "Thanks, guys."

"And gals." Laura gestured between her and Liv. "Don't forget us."

Blake picked up the lint-covered carrot and held it between two fingers like it was toxic sludge. "How could we?" He tossed it into a nearby trash can. "Things will be tough enough for Chase when he gets out without worrying about finding work. I appreciate you all being so open-minded."

Garrett scoffed, pushing to his feet and stretching his arms overhead. "Nothing to be open minded about where he's concerned."

"Exactly." Logan stood as well. "Chase will be a good addition to the team around here. Like a new member of the family."

"Yeah." Garrett directed his attention to Laura once

more. "Speaking of additions to the family, who's this Mike McQuade guy?"

She gave him and Liv both a deadly glare then grabbed her stuff and sprinted for the door like a cheetah on speed. She wasn't ready to talk about Mike with her family. Hell, she'd barely had time to think about this new thing with him herself and had no idea if it would even go anywhere. The last thing she wanted was the third degree from her siblings, good-natured though it was. "Got to go. Deadline."

"Right. Don't do anything we wouldn't do!" Her brothers called in unison as she fled down the hall to the exit.

She smiled all the way back to the Impala.

Doing anything with Mike suddenly sounded like the best idea in the world.

13

Fifteen minutes later, Laura pressed the Call button in the lobby of the Turnberry. She'd not intended to come back here again so soon. She'd intended to head home, change into her PJs, maybe do a final revision on her article for her editor J.J., then go to bed early. She wanted to get a good night's sleep before confronting her editor the next day about giving her the byline for her story. She'd earned it, dammit.

It was her time to shine, not do all the legwork for Dog Turd Davis.

Yet here she stood, eight-thirty at night, no guarantee Mike was even home, her pulse racing.

Maybe she should just leave, just forget about all of this, just chalk up this whole crazy attraction between them to exhaustion and bad decisions and move the hell on. Maybe she should just...

"Yes?" Mike's voice, low and slightly rough, oozed through the speaker. "Laura? What are you doing back here?"

She raised her hands to show the coffee and brownies she'd picked up at the 1020. "My meeting ended earlier, so I thought if you were free..."

He mumbled something under his breath that sounded suspiciously like a curse, and her heart tripped. Perhaps he wasn't alone. She hadn't considered the possibility before, but they'd never really discussed those areas of his life.

"Okay, fine." He buzzed her in, and the elevator doors swished open. "But I wasn't really prepared for guests tonight."

"Okay, no prob. I won't stay long, promise." She stepped in, and her stomach nosedived as the car lurched skyward. Considering the state of her own living quarters, she had no room to talk about anyone else's mess. Besides, the guy's place always looked pretty impeccable, at least from what she'd observed. How bad could things be?

The elevator dinged and the doors slid open, and she stepped off, fully prepared to assure him that the penthouse looked great, as always. Except, what she saw didn't look great. It looked...well, it looked incredible.

He cringed slightly at her speechless state and took the tray of coffee and food from her motionless hands. "Sorry. I warned you I wasn't prepared for guests."

Right.

What it appeared he *was* ready for was bed. He stood before her in nothing but a pair of plaid pajama pants and white tee-shirt. The tee-shirt was worn and a bit tight revealing his taut abs and muscled chest.

Her stomach clenched.

He set the coffee aside then lifted the same hand to scratch his fingers through his messy hair. In the other hand he held a toothbrush. "Uh, have a seat," he said, indicating the living room once more. "I'll just finish up in the bathroom. Be right back."

"Sure." She set her bag aside and shrugged out of her jacket then walked over to the floor-to-ceiling windows lining one wall. The lights of the Strip twinkled like jewels in the black-velvet night, and she took a deep breath before turning back to face the room.

Mike now stood on the other side of the room, sans toothbrush, watching her, his arms crossed. He padded back into the room and pulled a coffee from the tray. "Probably shouldn't be drinking this so late at night. I've got a busy day tomorrow."

"Me too." She walked over and pulled her cup out too. "I've got an interview with a one-hundred-five-year-old woman in the morning. She says video games have changed her life."

"Changed her life, huh?" He chuckled. "Did she lose her retirement savings buying them for her grandkids or something?"

"No." She smacked him on the arm then pulled away fast, her fingertips tingling from the brief contact. "She plays them herself. Won a few tourneys, too, from what her bio said."

"Seriously?" His eyes twinkled over the rim of his cup.

"Seriously." She shook her head and gave him a disparaging look. "Aren't you the one who's always touting how they're for players of all ages?"

"Yeah. I guess I am." A flicker of heat sparked through his warm brown gaze. "Want to sit?"

"Um." She glanced behind her at the couch, the scene of their earlier make out session, and moved toward the armchair instead. "Okay."

"Coward," he mumbled, so quietly she would've missed it if she wasn't so totally aware of him.

"I'm sorry?" Laura asked as she settled into her seat. "I didn't hear what you said."

"Nothing." His lips quirked into that sexy little half smile again. "Not important."

"All righty then." She leaned forward and grabbed one of the small plastic containers. "Brownie?"

"Sure. I never turn down chocolate." He passed her a napkin and fork, his fingers lingering against hers a tad longer than necessary. "Best baked goods ever."

"I know, right?" She opened her box and took a bite, but she could've been chewing on cardboard for all the attention she paid. All she could concentrate on was the way the sleek muscles of Mike's throat worked when he swallowed, the way he bit his lower lip as he relished the deep cocoa goodness of the brownie, the tiny crumb that clung to the corner of his mouth.

"You okay?" he asked, his tone laced with amusement. His gaze narrowed on her, the knowing look in his eyes far too perceptive.

"I'm fine." She stuffed another large bite of brownie into her mouth before she did something stupid, like melt into a puddle of goo at his feet. Would've worked, too, if she hadn't inhaled some of the powdered sugar sprinkled on top and started choking. Doubled over and eyes watering, she hacked her head off.

Way to be a lady, Laura.

Mike rushed to her side and pounded on her back. "Are you okay?"

She tried to talk, but her coughing interrupted.

Finally, she caught her breath and raised a hand to signal she was still alive, tears streaming down her face. Mike continued to rub her back as he crouched by her side. Even in her discombobulated state, the heat of him warmed her from the inside out.

"Laura?" he asked, pushing the hair away from her face and cupping her cheek. "Are you sure you're okay?"

She was many things at the moment—embarrassed, excited, enchanted—but okay wasn't one of them. She swallowed hard and nodded slowly, swiping the back of her hand over her wet cheek. Her answer croaked out of her abraded throat, bullfrog deep. "Yes."

"Yeah?" There it was again, that sexy smile. Was it her imagination or had he leaned in just a bit closer. "You sure?"

Her gaze dropped to his lips, to the way his tongue swept out to slick over his full bottom lip, the crumb still lingering on his skin. Without thought, she reached out and traced her finger over it, brushing away the crumb. "Positive."

"I do like a woman who's positive." He closed the small space between them and kissed her deeply.Irresistible.

Like she had it in her to resist. For once, she didn't even try.

LAURA WOKE ALONE in an unfamiliar bed to light streaming through the window. What time was it?

She rubbed her eyes and sat up, glancing at the clock. Ten a.m.

Shit.

Her interview was at noon.

The sound of the shower drifted in from her left, and she figured that's where Mike had gone. Pulling the sheet tighter around her, she got up and went in search of her clothes. Found her jeans and panties wadded up near the end of the bed then ventured out to the living room for her shirt and bra. She'd just made it back to the bedroom when Mike exited the bathroom, wearing a wet towel slung low around his hips and nothing else.

"Morning, Princess." He kissed her deeply then walked over to his dresser. "You might want to get dressed. Ted's due over here any second to work. You probably have time for a quick shower, though, if you want."

"Oh." She frowned. "Right. No. It's fine. I need to get home anyway. I've got my interview in a few hours."

"Granny gamer?" He chuckled.

"Yeah." Laura took a seat on the edge of the bed to pull on her panties and jeans, then stood to slip into her bra and shirt. At least things weren't as awkward between them this morning. One-nighters weren't her usual thing, but with Mike she couldn't resist.

From the other room, the elevator dinged. Now, she just needed to find her shoes and she'd be all set.

"I'm here," Ted called from the living room.

"Great." Mike yelled back to him then winked at Laura. He pulled open another drawer and yanked a fresh black T-shirt out of it. Before he closed it, she noticed a pile of disposable cell phones stuffed in one half of the space.

That was odd. Same brand as the one she'd seen in Troy's photo last week, too.

Then again, it was a popular brand. Millions of people probably used them.

Brushing off a slight niggle of concern, she searched the room for her socks and shoes then headed out into the living room again. Ted looked up from the open kitchen and caught her eyes, his expression surprised.

"Uh, hey," he said.

"Hey." Bingo. Shoes and socks located. She sat in the armchair to pull them on then gathered her bag and jacket as Mike walked into the room—shirt untucked, feet bare. "Well, I need to get going."

"Talk to you later?" Mike escorted her out to the elevators.

"Sure. You've got my number, right?"

"Always." He pressed the button then pulled her into his arms. "Last night really was amazing."

"Yeah, it kind of was, wasn't it?"

The elevator dinged and the door slid open, and he kissed her hard and fast. "Now go. Or else you won't be going anywhere for a long time, Princess."

She gave him a little wave then slumped against the back wall of the elevator as the doors slid closed. He waved back, one of those stupid burner phones clutched in his hand.

Nothing. The phone was nothing, she repeated to

herself all the way back to her car. Didn't matter that her instincts were rioting inside her.

Felicia was in police custody and Mike was innocent. Case closed.

No matter if her stupid reporter's gut told her something was still amiss.

14

Two days later, an irritating buzz woke Laura in the middle of the night. Okay, it was closer to seven in the morning, but still. This was the first time she'd slept in her own bed since the big night with Mike, and she was catching up on lost snooze.

She fumbled for her cell phone and answered it without checking the caller ID, her hair ratted and hanging in front of her face. "Hello?"

"I know you'll find out anyway and be a huge pain in my ass, so I figured I'd save us both the time and tell you. There's been a third victim."

Laura blew the hair out of her face and sat up. "Troy?"

"No. Killers R Us." His smartass response was followed up with a snort. "Who else would it be?"

"So there's another one?" She rubbed her eyes and yawned. "Where are they?"

"The Las Vegas Police Station."

Her eyes widened. "Oh my God. Someone staged a murder at the police station?"

"No." Troy sighed. "You haven't had your coffee yet, have you?"

"I haven't even brushed my teeth yet."

"Nice." She could hear the smile in his tone. "This one's still alive."

"Alive?" Laura straightened, her eyes wide, fully alert now. "That means you can question them and I can get an interview."

"Whoa there, cowgirl. One step at a time. Why don't you get up, get dressed, and get your cute butt down here first, then we'll see. And bring coffee with you. It's been a long night. Oh, and for the love of all things holy, brush your teeth."

She ignored his snide remarks and ended the call. After rushing through a quick shower and yes, brushing her teeth, she threw on a clean pair of jeans and a sweater, called the office to let them know she'd be in later than usual due to a lead, then hustled to the café then the police station.

Upon her arrival, Troy checked his watch then grabbed his drink from the tray. "One hour. I'm impressed, Rockford."

"Your approval is what I live for." Laura gave him a

simpering fake smile then cocked her chin toward his blackened left eye. "Make another new friend?"

"Haha. No. Arresting a perp. My face happened to get in the way of his fist."

Laura winced. It did look painful, all puffy and fifty shades of purple, red and yellowish green. Somehow, though, it only made him better looking, sort of rakish and rumpled. Too bad her affections were firmly fixed elsewhere these days. Troy Atkins would make some lucky woman quite happy someday. "So, tell me about this new victim."

Troy raised the hand holding his coffee and pointed with his index finger through a blind-covered window across from them. "His name's Steven Price. Thirty-eight."

"Huh." She moved closer to peer in at the guy. He sat in one of the smaller interrogation rooms, huddled beneath a blanket. Even though his shoulders were hunched, he looked like a linebacker—big and broad. His dark hair was slicked back in a similar hairstyle to that of the last victim at the Mob Museum and topped with a vintage fedora. She couldn't see the rest of his attire because of the blanket, but she'd bet his clothes were 1940s style, too. "Was he hurt?"

"Drugged, but otherwise unharmed. He's still a bit groggy, but the paramedics said whatever the attacker gave him should wear off completely in another hour or so. We questioned him already, but didn't get much."

"Can I talk to him?"

Troy took another long swig of coffee, watching her over the rim. Finally, he set his empty cup aside and stretched. "You know what? I'm feeling a little groggy myself. Think I'll take a stroll around the block to clear my head." He grabbed his jacket and headed for the door, turning toward her one last time. "So far Price hasn't declined questioning, but if he shows any resistance, please respect his decision."

"Got it. I won't push." She bit her lower lip. "Thanks, Troy."

He watched the tiny movement and frowned, his expression hovering between yearning and disappointment. "Yeah. You got thirty minutes, Rockford."

Once he left, Laura slipped into the interrogation room and closed the door behind her. She set the third coffee she'd picked up on the table in front of Price. He stared at it but didn't touch it.

She smiled and took a seat beside him, setting her messenger bag aside, then reaching into her pocket. "It's better than the sludge they have here. And there's some cream and sugar, if you take it."

Steven wrapped his beefy fingers around the cardboard cup. He didn't drink it, though he pulled it closer. His movements were slightly shaky. From the drugs or fear, she wasn't sure.

"Are you the sketch artist?" he asked. His rough voice sounded surprisingly small in the quiet room. "I told

Detective Atkins I don't remember much about the attack. When I came to, everything was sort of blurry. Then I popped the guy in the nose and got the hell out of there."

Laura's ears perked. "A man? Are you sure the attacker was male?"

Steven nodded and gave a short laugh. "Yeah. He might've screamed like a girl when I punched him, but he was a guy."

"Did you see his face?" She pulled out her trusty notebook and a pen, grinning. "Before you punched him, of course. Good job, there."

"Thanks." He toyed with the cup in his hands, turning it one way then the other, still unopened. "And no. I didn't see his face."

"What about other physical characteristics? Was he tall? Short? Fat? Thin?"

"On the thin side, I guess. A little shorter than me. It was hard to tell since I was either running away or on the ground."

"Where were you when you woke up?"

"Outside the Las Vegas Academy."

"Great." She scribbled her notes down. "And have you seen anybody following you lately? Anyone suspicious hanging around?"

"No." He scrunched his nose. "What does that have to do with you making a sketch?"

"Oh, nothing. Just trying to get some background to help set the scene."

"Listen, lady." He took off the fedora with a trembling hand, then stared at it like he hadn't been aware it was on his head. With a look of disgust, he tossed it aside. "I already told Detective Atkins this stuff. Can't you just ask him so I don't have to relive it all again?"

"Yeah, sure. Absolutely." She closed her notebook and pushed to her feet, snagging her messenger bag on the way to the door. "Thanks so much for your time, Mr. Price. Enjoy your coffee."

He grunted in response, his focus steadfast on the table.

Back in the hallway, Laura went in search of Troy and found him in his cubicle once more. She plopped down in the chair in front of his desk. "The perp's a man."

"Yep. That's what Price told me, too." He sighed and shook his head. "Damn. I really thought we had this one in the bag. But Felicia's been in our custody since yesterday, so we know she didn't do it."

"Maybe she did." She toyed with the end of her still-damp ponytail, eyes narrowed. "What if she has a partner?"

"Right. A partner like Mike McQuade."

"What?" Laura straightened, affronted on Mike's behalf. "No. He didn't do it."

"Really? How do you know?" He scowled and stared at her. She blushed and looked away. "That's quite a one eighty, Rockford. The other day you were ready to have me arrest him. What's the story there?"

"Nothing." She shifted in her seat and crossed her legs, her cheeks prickling with heat. "I've just talked to the guy a couple of times since then, and I don't think it's him."

"Because of your special reporter 'Spidey senses,' huh?" He gave her an irritated look. "Well, that guy's bad news, and I'd suggest you stay away from him."

"Yeah, 'cause you're so unbiased where I'm concerned." Laura crossed her arms. "Bad news how?"

"Bad news as in some...*questionable* things in his background."

"Questionable?"

He crooked a finger, inviting her over to his side of the desk. Once she moved in behind him, Troy clicked a few keys on his computer and brought up a video feed. "I shouldn't be showing you this, but..."

"Hey." Laura leaned closer. "That's footage from the foyer of Mike's penthouse, isn't it? How'd you get it?" Her brain raced through all the moments she and Mike had spent in that foyer, seeking any embarrassing behavior. The worst she could remember were a few heated kisses, thank goodness. The last thing she needed right now was the whole LVPD watching her and Mike's X-rated activities for shits and giggles. "Are you spying on him?"

"No. All legally obtained. I'm surprised you didn't know."

"Didn't know what?"

"Blake's company does all the security for McQuade. All I had to do was send a subpoena, and he turned it over to me."

Well, shit. At least that explained her oldest brother's odd look at her during the board meeting. She gave Troy some serious side eye then pointed at the screen again. "Isn't that the widow? Barbara Newton?"

"Yep." He tapped another key to play the video. "Watch this."

Barbara and Mike were in front of the elevator. Barbara appeared flustered, her hands flying about wildly as she said, "I think there's someone following me. I keep seeing the same figure—at work, at my house. My kids have seen him, too."

The camera was behind Mike, so she couldn't see his face, but he had his usual distracted tone, the one that drove Laura crazy. "Calm down," he said to Barbara, taking her arms. "Who do you think it might be?"

"I don't know." Barbara stared at the center of Mike's chest, her pretty face etched with sorrow. "Jim's death was an accident, right?"

"Of course it was." Mike rubbed the widow's arms affectionately, and Laura couldn't suppress a niggle of jealousy. Troubled, she clenched the back of Troy's chair tighter. This was stupid. Ridiculous. She was jealous of a dead woman. Still, she couldn't keep the thoughts of her meeting with Barbara's kids out of her head. Had Mike and Barbara been lovers? The way he touched her on the video suggested a familiarity beyond platonic, but...

Shaking off her doubts, she concentrated on the footage again. If she had questions, she'd just ask him later. After all, they were spending a lot of time together lately. That afforded her some privileges where his past was concerned.

Onscreen, Barbara continued questioning Mike, her panic evident in her voice. "But what if it wasn't? What if someone killed my Jim and now they're coming for me?"

Before Mike answered, another figure appeared in the frame: Ted, his posture hunched and his eyes twitchy. Mike looked irritated at the interruption, startled almost. *Maybe he didn't want any witnesses to his conversation with Barbara?*

Ted stood to the side of Mike and Barbara, pointing off screen to what Laura knew was the living room. "I, uh, finished that, uh, coding, boss. If you, uh, want to take a look..."

Mike gave the guy a dismissive nod then waited for him to leave before turning his attention back to Barbara. "Listen, I know the anniversary of Jim's death is coming up. I can't imagine how hard that must be for you and the kids, and I'm sorry you have to go through that, but I really think you're letting your imagination get the better of you." He wrapped his arm around Barbara's shoulders and pressed the button for the elevator. From his now visible expression—flat, slightly annoyed—

Laura would almost think he was blowing the widow's concerns off. But why would he do that to someone he obviously cared about?

It made no sense.

The elevator doors slid open, and he helped Barbara in, his polite smile the polar opposite of his tense tone. "Promise me you'll find a way to relax. No one will hurt you. I promise."

Troy hit another key on his keyboard, and the computer screen went black as he swiveled his chair to face her. "I rest my case."

Laura scoffed. "That video doesn't prove anything."

"Hmm." Troy leaned back and clasped his hands over his flat stomach. "Proves you haven't told me the complete truth. This isn't the only tape we got from your brother. Turns out you're in quite a few of them."

"My association with Mike McQuade is private."

"Not around here it isn't. Or at least it won't be, if one of the other officers gets ahold of these tapes. For now, I've managed to keep a lid on them. Can't guarantee that will always be the case, though."

Her anger rose at his veiled threat. "What exactly are you suggesting, Detective Atkins?"

"What I'm suggesting, Ms. Rockford, is that you stop hanging around with McQuade." His cool smile made her blood boil. If they weren't there, in the middle of the station, she'd show him just how much he'd pissed her off with a nice kick in the pants. She'd thought Troy was her friend, a nice guy she'd perhaps go on a date with sometime. Except nice guys didn't blackmail their friends. She wondered what other secrets golden-boy Troy might have hidden under his slick, cover-model persona.

He continued, seemingly unfazed by her growing fury. "Mike McQuade is bad news. That video proves there's more to his relationship with Barbara Newton. Not to mention the incidents in his past that—"

"Hey, Atkins," another detective called from across the room. "Can we let Price go home now?"

Troy stood and brushed past Laura, then leaned closer to whisper in her ear. "Stay away from him, Rockford. Or else."

Livid, Laura waited until he'd gone back into the interrogation room before she grabbed her stuff and left. *Or else what?* He'd show those tapes to his buddies on the force and make her look like a lying slut in front of the whole police department? He'd ruin her reputation and her sources in Vegas? What an asshole. She pushed outside and headed for her Impala.

After shoving her bag onto the passenger seat, Laura climbed in behind the wheel and cranked the engine. Why the hell was Troy digging into Mike's past so hard anyway? It was almost like he *wanted* to find something wrong, like he didn't want to shine the spotlight elsewhere, like maybe Troy might have something to do with it all...

Her breath hitched. *Oh, God.* Where had *that* come from? But as she backed out of her parking spot and thought about it more, it kind of made sense. Troy would certainly have the access, being a cop and all. Not to mention the fact he seemed to have some personal vendetta against Mike McQuade all of a sudden.

Distracted, she headed back downtown toward the Turnberry, wondering about Troy's last crack concerning incidents in Mike's past.

She'd come clean to Mike about her documentary ruse. Now it was his turn. Time for him to tell her the truth about his past.

15

By ten-fifteen, Laura stood in the Turnberry's lobby once more, buzzing Mike's penthouse. Incensed, she stepped back and stared up into the little security camera on the wall, tapping her toe while she waited for him to answer.

"Yeah?" The deep timbre of Mike's voice over the intercom reminded her of lazy Sunday mornings in bed, but she refused to be distracted. "Who's there?"

"It's me." She stepped into the camera's range. "Can I come up?"

Mike chuckled. "Of course." Then, perhaps reading her mood, his tone sobered. "Something wrong?"

"We need to talk."

She rode up, muscles tense and mind stewing. By the time the doors slid open and Mike pulled her into a hug, she'd worked herself into a fine snit. Laura remained stiff in his embrace, and he pulled back, frowning down at her. "What's wrong?"

"Nothing." She blinked up at him then pushed him away. "No bruises."

"Excuse me?"

"No one's punched you in the face. That's good."

"I like to think so." He followed her into the living room, looking as confused as she felt. She started to sit on the sofa, then decided at the last minute not to—she didn't want him to sit too close.

In the end she stood in front of the windows, having dismissed sitting altogether. It was a better tactical move anyway. If he did turn out to be the murderer after all, or if he said something she didn't like, being on her feet already made for easier bolting.

Mike stood off to the side, watching her entire performance with amusement. "So, what do we need to talk about?"

"I was at the police station earlier. They had video. Of you. And the first victim, the widow, Barbara Newton. Here, in your penthouse. Things looked rather...*cozy*."

"Cozy?" He stood perfectly still, inscrutable as always.

"Yeah. She told you she thought someone was following her, but you didn't believe her. Why?"

"I don't remember." His warm brown eyes narrowed. "It was a long time ago."

"But you do remember her?"

"Of course I remember her. Her husband used to work for me. What's not to remember?"

"You're hiding something." Laura compressed her lips, refusing to look away from him. "I know it."

"What exactly is happening here, Laura?" He moved closer to her. "What exactly are you accusing me of?"

"I'm not sure yet."

"I see." He stood before her now at the windows, hands on his hips, lips tight. "I didn't kill Jim, if that's what you're getting at. It was an accident. I've never killed anyone, actually. Though it sounds like that's what you think happened."

"I don't know what to think, Mike. You don't tell me anything."

He exhaled, scowling at the floor for a moment before taking her arm and guiding her over to a long chaise lounge next to the far wall. "Sit down and I'll tell you everything that's in my power to tell, okay? Let me just make us some coffee first. I haven't had any yet today, and you know how I am without my caffeine fix."

"Right. So you can slip some poison in there or something? No thanks." The taunt sounded childish even to her, but dammit. He made her so mad with all his hidden facets and dark secrets. It was her job to read people, to learn their worst, but he defied all of her rules.

"Seriously?" He gave her an aggravated, slightly pained look. "Look, if I wanted to do you in, I sure as hell wouldn't use poison. Too traceable. And why would I do it here? In my house? Do you know how much blood removal costs these days?"

"No, I don't, but apparently you do, huh? And are you saying you *do* want to do me in, just by different methods?" She crossed her arms again, her expression mulish. "Nice. Tell me, what exactly is the going rate for blood removal?"

"It was a joke." Finally, she'd gotten a rise out of him. Laura sighed. "Just make the damned coffee."

"Fine." He stomped from the room.

"Fine," she yelled at his retreating back, to get the last word. Alone in the living room, she plunked her bag down at her feet then stared at her toes. A series of bangs and curses issued from the direction of the kitchen, and her curiosity got the better of her. She couldn't resist investigating. With a shoulder propped against the door frame, she watched Mike fumble around for the ingredients. "Do you have any idea what you're doing?"

"No."

Exhaling loudly, she pushed him out of the way and took the pack of filters from his hand. "Let me do it."

He glowered at her while she shoved a filter into the basket then scooped in some coffee. As she filled the carafe with water, she couldn't take his stony silence anymore. "So, tell me how this Jim Newton died."

He ran a hand through his disheveled hair and leaned his hip against the counter. "He was my head programmer. We were all here, at the penthouse, for the release party for *Vegas Noir*. It was M Cubed's first game and kind of a big deal. I don't know exactly what took place, but Jim went out on the balcony for some air. Next thing I knew, he was floating face down in the pool, dead." He closed his eyes and shook his head. "The police report said he'd had too much to drink and fell in. Drowned. The coroner's report corroborated those findings. They ruled it an accident. Some celebration, huh?"

Despite her wariness, Mike looked like someone had kicked his puppy, and Laura couldn't stop herself from comforting him. She pushed Start on the coffee machine then laid a hand on his forearm. "I'm sorry."

He stared at the floor. "He was my best friend. We were going to build this company together."

Troy's warnings from earlier came back to her mind, along with the widow's panicked statement. "Is there any reason to suspect it wasn't an accident?"

"I don't know anymore. It was five years ago, Laura." Mike sighed. "With all these new murders happening, I don't know what to think."

Not wanting to take advantage of his vulnerable state but not wanting to back off either, Laura pushed a bit more. "When I went out to talk to Barbara Newton's kids, they told me you gave their mother money every month."

Silence. His only movement was a muscle twitching near his clenched jaw.

If Mike had been involved with Jim's widow sexually,

she needed to know. She might be lonely and like him more than she cared to admit, but she sure as hell wouldn't climb in bed with a man who'd just lost his lover, possibly by his own hand. "Want to tell me why you'd do that?"

Seconds ticked by with agonizing slowness. At last, Mike cursed under his breath and stared out the window over the sink. "Jim's life insurance only covered the funeral expenses. I'm godfather to those kids. I couldn't leave them with nothing. I know what that's like, growing up poor, always wanting, always having to work and prove yourself for every damned thing. They deserved better." His brow furrowed, and his bare toes curled on the tile floor. "Besides, if it wasn't for me throwing that stupid party, Jim might still be alive."

"It wasn't your fault, Mike." Laura inched closer. "You can't blame yourself."

"Yeah." He laughed, hollow and unpleasant. "I've been telling myself that for five fucking years. Maybe someday I'll believe it."

"Mike, I—"

The coffee maker beeped, severing her speech. She located two mugs in a cupboard he indicated. After she poured them each a cup and handed him one, they made their way back to the living room and settled on the chaise again. "That must've been what Troy meant about your dark past."

"My what?" He took a sip from his mug then wrinkled his nose. "And who's Troy?"

"A homicide detective on the force."

"Ah. Blake investigated Jim's case, you know."

Laura frowned. Blake hadn't mentioned that.

"No, I didn't know that. But that timeline makes sense." She took a sip of her own coffee and gagged. "God, this stuff tastes like crap."

"Yeah." He tried another gulp and cringed. "Definitely not your best work. Maybe *you're* trying to poison *me*, huh?"

Laura laughed then set the cup aside. "Maybe. Sorry. So why don't you have your usual brew from 1020 today?"

Mike placed his mug next to Laura's on the table. "Ted usually does the morning coffee run on his way in, but he called in sick today."

"Oh." She looked around, realizing, not for the first time, just how adorable he looked in the morning, all rumpled and sleepy. "Guess that means he won't be popping in to disturb us like he usually does, huh?"

Mike traced his hand up her back to cup the nape of her neck and draw her closer. "Nope. No disturbances today."

LAURA HAD BEEN all Mike could think of since the last

time they'd been together. They'd both tried to pretend it was casual, a one-time thing, but Mike knew it wasn't that way for him. Laura was different than the other women who'd previously graced his bed. She was smart and funny and quirky, not to mention unbelievably hot. He couldn't seem to get enough of her and now that she was in his arms, he didn't want to let her go.

She looked up at him, her hazel eyes half closed. "No more secrets between us, Mike."

"No more secrets." He kissed her gently. "No more."

A niggling urge to check the clock gripped him, but he brushed it aside. For once, the world could survive without him. He pulled Laura closer, trying not to think about the promise still echoing in the air.

So, his princess had investigated him, and she'd returned to him anyway. His hopes for a future between them flared brighter. Hell, today he'd come right out and told her what a crappy human being he was, and yet she'd stayed. A pang of guilt shot through him, but he kissed her until it dissolved. He'd promised no more secrets, but there was one thing he could never tell her— one secret he'd have to keep. He pushed the thought aside. *That* secret had no bearing on what was happening now.

For once, he had everything he needed right here.

For once, he held goodness in his arms and felt like maybe he actually deserved it.

16

The next afternoon, Mike was going over the latest game configurations with Ted at the penthouse when the security buzzer rang.

"Expecting someone?" Ted asked, his voice sounding more nasal than usual from the cold. Mike had wanted him to take more time off, but Ted had insisted on coming over today. Like Mike, Ted was a workaholic.

"No. Wasn't expecting anyone, actually." Mike got up and walked over to the security panel in the foyer. His other staff worked at the main office, and Laura was off doing another one of her human-interest pieces, a kid who collected asteroids or something, she'd said. He pressed the button and did his best to keep his irritation from his tone. He hated most interruptions, and they really needed to get these games ready for production by the end of the week. "Yes?"

"Hey, Big Bro." Reba gave a little wave into the camera. "Got a minute?"

Mike glanced back at Ted then sighed. "Come on up, but make it fast. I'm behind schedule."

"Whatever."

The elevator doors slid open moments later. His little sister stepped out and grabbed him in a tight hug, the top of her head several inches below his chin. They shared the same dark coloring, the same cautious personalities, the same secrets.

"To what do I owe this honor?" he asked, pulling away.

"I heard there was another attempted murder with a scene like your game."

"Yeah." Mike wrapped an arm around her shoulders and led her into the living room. "Ted, you remember my little sister Reba?"

The guy gave a slight nod, then focused his attention right back on his paperwork.

"C'mon." Mike led Reba into the kitchen then took a seat beside her at the island. "I saw the story on the local news this morning. You want something to drink?"

"Nah, I'm fine." She tapped her fingers on the granite countertop. "It's creepy, right?"

"Yep, it's disturbing. Not sure why anyone would do that."

Reba pursed her lips. "I'm worried."

"Why?" Mike took her hand, frowning as she trembled.

She leaned closer, her voice low. "What if the police start digging into what happened with Lyle again?"

"They won't. Why would they? This is just some obsessed weirdo acting out. Besides, there's nothing even connecting this last guy to me or the company. They won't reopen Lyle's case."

His sister gave him an incredulous look. "Uh, the latest victim is Steven Price."

"So?"

"So he's the boyfriend of Gloria Reyes." When Mike still had no idea who the guy was, Reba swatted him hard on the arm. "From your accounting department."

"Oh." The company had grown so fast over the last few years that he had a hard time keeping track of all the new faces, but yeah. Now that Reba mentioned accounting, he remembered the pretty Latina woman who balanced his books. "That's her boyfriend, huh?"

Ted walked in and headed straight for the coffee pot. "You guys talking about that new victim?"

"Yeah," Mike said, glancing at Reba. "Guess he dates some gal in our accounting office."

Ted gave him a disapproving look. "You don't remember that? You used to remember everyone who worked for you."

"Things used to be a lot smaller and less complicated

than they are now, too." Mike rubbed his face. "Guess I need to start paying attention again."

"Guess maybe you do," Ted said quietly before taking his coffee back into the other room.

Mike shook his head to clear the feelings of guilt. Had he become one of those CEO's that didn't care about his people? He'd have to remedy that. He looked at Reba and smiled. "You want to take a walk or something?"

"Can't, sorry." She hopped off her stool. "I'm meeting a friend in ten minutes for mani-pedis. I just wanted to make sure you knew about what was going on and to warn you to be careful. If they dig into that case, it might not be good for you. Promise me if you hear something about Lyle, you'll let me know?"

"Of course." He walked her back to the elevator. "You sure you're okay?"

She rose on tiptoe and kissed his cheek then stepped into the elevator. "Yeah, I'm okay. See you around."

"See ya." Mike kept the smile on his face as he watched the elevator door close on his little sister, but it faded as he turned back to his apartment. What had happened with Lyle Kennedy shouldn't worry him. It was done. Over with. Case closed. But Reba had a point about the police digging into Lyle's death again in light of these new murders. One never knew how the police were going to twist evidence to suit their agenda.

LATE THAT NIGHT, Laura pulled into a spot one street over and several blocks from her building and exited the Impala. Normally, she parked closer, but everything was taken. Must be some special concert or something going on tonight. Oh, well. The weather was warm, and she needed the exercise anyway after sitting on her butt all morning interviewing that kid. The article had then taken way longer to write and edit than she'd expected, but at least it was done. With any luck, she wouldn't have too many more of those human-interest pieces in her future.

She waited at the light to cross the street, the area just as crowded at eleven thirty p.m. as it was at eleven thirty a.m. Tourists poured in and out of the casinos and nightclubs, and the neon signs cast a pretty rainbow glow on the pavement.

Green light flashing, Laura continued on down the sidewalk and stepped aside to dodge what appeared to be a group of intoxicated women at a bachelorette party. One of the gals went crazy over a life-sized cutout of a male stripper from one of the nearby bars' revues, and Laura chuckled.

A block ahead, she turned the corner. One more block to her building. She'd thought about calling Mike to see if he wanted to come over, but she knew how busy he was with his new games getting ready for release. Besides, after the day she'd had, a night alone sounded pretty good right now. She stopped suddenly and rubbed the back of her neck. Her skin prickled, and she glanced behind her, the weight of a stare heavy on her shoulders, though she spotted no one other than the usual tourists.

To be on the safe side, she reached into the side pocket of her messenger bag and gripped the small can of mace she always kept there. The streets of Vegas were fairly safe at any hour, but it never hurt to be prepared.

As she got closer to her apartment, the crowds started to thin out. Still, she couldn't shake the feeling that someone was watching her, following her. Laura pulled out her phone and clicked it on, then hesitated. Who would she call? Worse, what proof did she have? Just her gut instincts, which, accurate though they usually were, weren't exactly hard evidence.

Moonlight cast long shadows all around her, broken here and there by the orange glow of the streetlights. She looked behind her again and thought she spotted someone in a hoodie dart into a doorway.

Mike always wears hoodies...

Stop it.

Mike wasn't the killer. They'd shared everything the other night. She trusted him.

It wasn't Mike.

She turned another corner, walked a few steps, and looked behind her.

No one.

Laura sighed. she was being ridiculous. Letting all the murders get to her. No one was behind her. Still, she couldn't shake the feeling of someone watching her. Not behind her now, though, up ahead toward her apartment.

The phone rested heavy in her palm. Maybe she could call Troy. There wasn't anything the police could do without a credible threat of violence, but still. He'd probably at least do a friendly drive-by for her.

Her apartment building loomed in the distance, still half a block ahead.

No. She could handle this by herself. If someone approached, she'd bust out all the self-defense skills Liv had taught her. No big deal. Her thumb hovered over the keypad. Then again, there was always Mike. His penthouse was only a few blocks farther than her place. And he could be here sooner than Troy, if necessary.

Cursing, she shoved the phone back into her pocket and quickened her steps. This was stupid. She was a grown, capable woman. She didn't need to run to a man to fix her problems, even one as cute and cuddly as her Mike.

Her Mike?

Distracted, she barged ahead and ran smack into a hard, muscled male chest.

Laura blinked up into the face of the man she'd damned near mowed down and frowned. "Troy? What are you doing here? Are you following me?"

"No." He released her and stepped back, the bruise

from his black eye looking dark in the streetlight. "I was coming from a crime scene."

"Another game-related victim?" Laura did her best to ignore the rush of panic those words created in her system. If there'd been another body found, this one was close to her home. Far too close for her comfort. Never a good sign. And if someone was stalking her... The widow had feared she'd had a stalker, too...

"No." Troy narrowed his gaze on her. "You look like you've seen a ghost. You okay?"

"I'm fine." She took a deep breath. "Just stressed and tired."

"Bad day?"

"Bingo."

He thrust his hands into his pockets and rocked back on his heels. "You want to grab a drink or something? I'm off duty now."

"No." He raised his brows at her snippy tone and she winced. "Sorry. Don't think I'd be very good company tonight. I'll just head home and go to bed."

"Alone?"

"Excuse me?" She bristled under his nosiness. "That's none of your business."

Laura peered into the distance. She didn't see any blinking lights or crime scene. Since when did cops *walk* to a crime scene? The thought briefly crossed her mind that Troy was the one watching her, then she dismissed it. Cops didn't stalk people, did they?

She started walking toward her apartment building again and he kept pace beside her. "As long as it isn't McQuade, we're good. I'm telling you, Laura, that guy is bad news."

"This from the guy who tried to blackmail me the other day." She glared at him. "Sorry, but I think I'll make my own decisions on who's best for me."

"Hey, look. I'm sorry. I never meant to threaten you, Laura. It's just..." He raked a hand through his thick blond hair and swore under his breath. "I care about you, okay? I don't want to see you get hurt, and I know you've been back to see him."

"Are you spying on me now?" She gave him some serious side eye. "Because if you are, I'll report you to your superiors, Atkins."

"No. The security feeds, remember? Blake's still sending them over every night. I saw you on there again a few days ago."

"Where exactly *are* these cameras in Mike's place?"

"Main lobby and penthouse foyer." He held up his hands in surrender. "That's it. I swear."

"Better be." They stopped in front of her apartment building. "Mike told me about what happened with the widow's husband, Jim. He's told me everything, and I'm okay with it, so just stop trying to interfere, all right?"

Troy gave her a pointed stare. "He told you he's been accused of murder before?"

"The drowning at his penthouse was ruled an accident. I looked it up myself to confirm."

"I'm not talking about the drowning."

Dread congealed in the pit of her stomach. "What *are* you talking about?"

"Lyle Kennedy."

"Never heard of him."

"It was a while ago, but you should look that one up too, Laura. Lot of people think he got away with killing that guy, just like he's getting away with killing these people now." He stepped closer to her and lowered his voice to a conspiratorial whisper. "And we found something else, too."

She swallowed hard. "What?"

"At the first crime scene. A disposable phone. We think it connects back to Mike."

"I need to go." She rushed up the front stoop and opened the door. "Goodbye, Troy."

"Look up Kennedy, Laura. Make your own decision."

As she rode up to her apartment, Laura slumped against the wall of the elevator, more exhausted than she'd ever remembered. Mike had promised her no more secrets. Now this. Lyle Kennedy she could look up easily enough, but the cell phone? She'd seen Mike's stash of phones firsthand and had made the connection herself that they were the same brand as the one in the picture on Troy's desk right after the widow's murder.

Dammit.

She was so sick of the men in her life running roughshod. Determined, she waited until the doors opened but didn't exit. Instead, she pressed the button for the first floor again and rode back down to the lobby. Back outside, she turned and headed in the direction of the Turnberry.

Ten minutes later, she stood in front of the security camera in Mike's lobby, jamming the Call button.

He answered on the fourth buzz. "What?"

"I have some more questions for you, mister."

"Now?"

"Hell yes, now."

Seconds later, Laura stormed off the elevator in his foyer, doing her best not to stare at his broad, naked chest or the way his boxers clung lovingly to his hips. "How can we possibly have a serious relationship if you don't tell me the truth?"

He scratched his chin and rubbed his eyes. "We're having a serious relationship?"

"Pay attention." She tossed her bag into the living room then stood before him, hands on her hips. "Did you kill Barbara Newton?"

"What?" He scrunched his nose. "No! How can you even say that?"

"Because I saw all those disposable phones in your bedroom, and the police found one just like it at the first crime scene. They said they can connect it to you."

"Seriously? A cheap burner phone is what makes you

think I'm a murderer?" He cursed and turned away. "Jesus, Laura. Millions of people use those same phones. I use them because crazy fans keep hacking into my computers and my Internet lines and figuring out my phone number. If I didn't use disposable phones, I'd have no privacy at all."

Damn. His explanation sounded completely rational, and the stricken look on his face made her want to hold him and tell him everything would be fine. But she couldn't do that.

Not yet.

"What about Lyle Kennedy?"

Mike's attention snapped to her. "Excuse me?"

"Troy, my detective friend. He mentioned him to me earlier. Said you were accused of murdering him, too."

"Shit, Laura." A vein near his temple pulsed. "I can't talk about that."

"Can't or won't?" She waited, tapping her toe against the tile, but he didn't answer. "Fine. That's fine, Mike." Grabbing her bag, Laura stalked back to the elevator and jabbed the button with an angry finger. "You know what? Forget it. Keep your damned secrets and forget about me, okay?"

She stepped aboard and the doors started to close, but Mike thrust his hand inside. "Laura, wait. I—"

Furious and hurt, she pressed the lobby button over and over ignoring him until he removed his hand and the doors slid shut. She should've known better than to let her heart lead over her head. Arms crossed, she blinked back tears. To think she'd thought they'd had something special. She'd even considered inviting Mike over to Blake's for the next Rockford family dinner. Thank God *that* hadn't happened. She could just imagine the look on her brothers' faces when she introduced her latest boyfriend and he turned out to be a murderer. She'd never had the best luck with men, but at least none of her previous dates had a body count.

Downstairs, she charged out of the Turnberry and brushed the tears off her cheeks.

Maybe this was all for the best anyway. She didn't need a relationship. Now she could concentrate on her career, get that big scoop she'd dreamed of, move on to bigger and better journalism. Best of all, she'd gotten away from Mike before she'd become his next victim, murderous or otherwise.

***

*S*HIT. *Shit. Shit.*

Mike pounded his fist into the wall beside the elevator. He should have told Laura everything, he should've told her the truth, he should've run after her and begged her to come back.

Only problem was, it wasn't his truth to tell.

Exhaling loud, he stalked back in the dark living room and fisted his hands in his hair. *Figures.* He finally met a woman he saw a future with and she left him over the one thing he couldn't change.

His past.

Fuck.

He grabbed his phone and dialed Reba's number. This late, she was probably in bed, as he'd been before Laura showed up again and accused him of murder. Again. A familiar ache cramped his chest, the ache he got whenever he was apart from Laura these days.

Dammit. He couldn't lose her, not over a lie.

His sister's voicemail picked up on the fourth ring, and he left a brief message about needing to see her the next day. After he ended the call, Mike sank down onto the chaise lounge and stared out his pristine windows, over the pool where his best friend had perished, into the twinkling light of Vegas beyond. The day before, he and Laura had had something that might have lasted a lifetime.

Now, she was gone, perhaps forever.

No. He shook his head and inhaled sharply, squeezing the cheap phone in his hand so tightly the plastic cracked. He couldn't carry this burden. Not anymore.

It's time.

Time to come clean.

Come clean with Laura and deal with the ramifications of his past sins, for better or worse.

17

———

Early the next morning, Laura opened her apartment door to grab her daily edition of the *Chronicle* and instead discovered a beautiful bouquet of red roses. Roses were her favorite. Probably from Mike, she supposed, as she picked up the crystal vase and stepped back inside.

Surrounded by the heady fragrance of fresh flowers, she shut the door with her hip then studied the arrangement. Velvety red blooms, pristine white baby's breath, lush green leaves. Gorgeous. The guy probably felt guilty for being such a lying schmuck, as he should.

As if a floral arrangement would make her forgive him. Or would it? Maybe she had overreacted about Lyle Kennedy? She and Mike had only known each other a short time, and she couldn't expect him to tell her *every-thing* about his past. Yet Troy had said Mike had been accused of killing Kennedy. *Murder*? Shouldn't he have mentioned that?

But he couldn't be guilty. Something deep inside her told her Mike was no murderer, and besides, he was still walking the streets, so he hadn't been convicted of killing Kennedy. Her instincts about people were usually spot on, and they'd told her Mike was a good man. Not a killer. She never would have slept with a killer ... unless her overactive hormones had put the kibosh on all her warning signals.

She sighed and searched through the blooms for a card. Her fingers brushed against something solid and soft inside the fragrant flowers, and Laura frowned.

Not a card. Definitely not a card.

She pulled out the object and gasped. A small black velvet box. She creaked open the lid and discovered a diamond engagement ring nestled on a tiny bed of black satin. Hands trembling, she set the flowers on the counter and peered more closely at the ring. No jeweler's mark she could find in the tiny box, which meant most likely it was a fake, but still. After their argument last night, no way would Mike send her an engagement ring. And even if they hadn't fought, they'd only known each other a few weeks. Hell, he hadn't even met her family yet, or she his.

Images from the previous night flashed back into her mind. The feeling of being watched, the shadowy figure in the hoodie ducking into the shadows, the claustrophobic feeling of having nowhere to run...

A knock sounded on the door, and she jumped.

It wasn't even seven yet, and she wasn't expecting anyone. Her phone buzzed on the counter again, and she swallowed hard. Mike must've sent her at least twenty voicemails and texts since she'd stormed out of his place. She hadn't answered any of them, and she sure as hell wasn't about to start now.

All she wanted was for this whole damned fiasco to be over so she could move on.

The pounding on her door grew more insistent, and her heart tumbled, her pulse pounding loud in her head. What if she *did* have a stalker? And what if it was him or her outside her door? What if....

"Laura, if you're in there, please open up."

Mike.

Laura wasn't sure if she should be relieved or terrified. He'd never been to her apartment, though he knew where she lived. Hell, with all his Internet skills, he probably knew how many fillings she had in her teeth and what size gym shoe she wore in the fifth grade.

Squaring her shoulders, she clicked the small black box closed and shoved it into a nearby kitchen drawer. Time to put her big girl panties on and deal with the situation. Liv had taught her well. If Mike tried something with her today, she'd kick his ass into next week.

Simple.

Except when she opened the door and saw him there, looking thoroughly disheveled and sleepy and stubbly from lack of shaving, all she wanted to do was pull him into her arms and ease the lines of tension around his beautiful eyes and mouth.

No. She forced her warm fuzzy thoughts to the wayside. Mike had an uncanny knack for showing up wherever she happened to be. Too uncanny, in her opinion. Which meant he was either a psychic, which she doubted, or he was following her. Stalking her, to be more precise.

Careful.

She pulled open the door a few inches, keeping her privacy chain intact. Teeth clenched, she forewent polite greetings. "What are you doing here?"

"Why haven't you returned my messages?"

"Maybe because it's six in the damned morning?" She met his stony glare with one of her own. "And maybe I don't want to talk to you anymore. Pretty sure I made that clear last night."

"Too bad." Mike's narrowed gaze dropped from her eyes to her lips. "We need to talk."

"Why? So you can lie to me again? No thanks." She started to close the door, but he shoved his arm inside.

"Please, Laura. Don't do this. We had something special happening between us." His tone turned plaintive, and her heart pinched. "At least I thought we did.

Please just listen to me. I promise I'll tell you everything this time."

Part of her wanted to listen, so badly it hurt. But the other part of her, the part that had been kicked to the curb one too many times in the past, urged caution. "You said you'd tell me everything last time too. You didn't."

"Look, please. There are things that—"

"If you tell me once more there are things I don't understand, I will hurt you. Be warned."

"Fine." He sighed. "I just... I don't want to lose you, Laura. Can I at least come in?"

She glanced down at her rumpled PJs then around her messy living quarters. Not exactly the perfectly maintained penthouse he lived in, but who cared. Wasn't like she was trying to impress the guy anymore anyway. "Fine."

Laura unchained the door and stepped aside.

Mike walked in and glanced around. "Thanks, for uh, talking to me."

She crossed her arms and scowled. "Hurry up. I've got to get ready for work. Some of us are trying to build a career here."

"I know all about building a career, Laura. I built M Cubed from the ground up, remember? But there's more to life than just work." His attention caught on the bouquet on the kitchen counter. "Nice flowers."

"Thanks. You would think so, since you sent them."

"Me?" He wrinkled his nose. "While I'd like to take credit, it wasn't me."

"Really? And I suppose you didn't send the ring either, huh?" She stalked into the kitchen and yanked the small box out of the drawer, on a roll now. "You know, that really takes some balls, mister. Especially considering I cut you loose last night."

"Ring? What the hell are you talking about, Laura? I mean, I like you a lot. More than a lot, but I don't think we're quite there yet, do you?"

"Well, somebody thinks so." She opened the little box and thrust it in front of him. "It's not even real."

He took it from her and studied it closely. "This didn't come from me. When I give you a ring, it will be one hundred percent real. And bigger. Much bigger than this. You deserve only the best, Laura."

"Stop it." She snatched the box back from him and tossed it on the counter. "We are not together anymore, and I think it's time we both accept that and move the hell on."

"You really have no idea who sent that ring or those flowers?"

"I thought I did." She gave him a pointed stare. "Still not convinced it wasn't you."

"Not me, I swear." He crossed his heart for emphasis. "Have you gotten anything else weird like that?"

"No." She crossed her arms again. Like she'd tell him anyway. Wasn't any of his business. He was probably jealous, trying to scope out her other dating options. "Why?"

"Unfortunately, I've had plenty of experience with stalkers, Laura. You might want to mention something to the police. You said you have friends on the force, right?"

She nodded.

"They can't do much with just some flowers and a ring, but at least they can take a report. That way you'll have something on record if it happens again."

The last thing she wanted this morning was to stand here discussing the do's and don'ts of stalking etiquette in her PJs, hair a mess, no makeup, with the man she was still half in love with despite the fact she'd broken up with him the night before. Her irritation won out over common sense, and she said the first hateful words that came to mind, knowing there was no proof they were true, knowing they'd hurt him. "You'd like that, wouldn't you? Maybe get another notch on your killer bedpost, huh? Do all those police reports against you up your street cred, Mike?"

He opened his mouth. Closed it. "You know what, forget it. Forget I came here today. Forget I tried to help you, protect you. Goodbye, Laura." He yanked the door open and walked out, not bothering to close it behind him.

Pissed, she leaned out into the hall and yelled at his retreating back. "Goodbye, Mike. And I mean it this time."

He didn't turn around.

She slammed the door behind her then leaned against it, sliding down to the hardwood floor. She felt worse than she had before, if that were possible. Mike was well and truly gone. The one man she'd fallen for so hard and so fast. Gone.

The roses mocked her from the kitchen counter.

Mike said he hadn't sent the flowers, but he was likely a liar and possibly a murderer. On the other hand, if he wasn't and they really weren't from him, then who were they from?

Needing something to distract her from the black hole that had swallowed her heart and threatened to engulf her whole world, she pushed to her feet and padded back into the open galley kitchen. There had to be something, some identifying mark on the bouquet somewhere. She pulled the flowers apart and finally found a small sticker stuck on the back of the iridescent ribbon tied around the vase in a pretty bow. Riegler's Florists, Henderson, Nevada.

Henderson.

That's where Barbara Newton and her kids had lived.

She closed her eyes and pictured that day at their house. The room, somewhat untidy from two teenagers living there basically alone. The somber tone. The bouquet, the same as this one, sitting on a table against the wall.

Oh, shit.

Her eyes flew open, and Laura gripped the counter tight.

The flowers and the ring were from the killer.

MIKE TOOK the stairs down to the first floor, needing the time and exercise to get his shit together. The fact Laura had dismissed him from her life, again, was bad enough. Then there was the small detail that she thought he was some psycho serial killer.

Fuck.

Fuck, fuck, fuck.

Maybe there was a reason he was thirty-three and still single. Maybe he didn't date because it was a hell of a lot safer to have your heart locked away than to get it pulverized by people you loved who didn't love you back.

Loved?

His footsteps faltered, and he stopped somewhere between the third and second floors, gripping the railing tight. Love Laura? He couldn't seem to stop thinking about her, even when he was working, which never happened. He couldn't seem to keep from hoping she was okay, that she was happy, that she might be thinking about him, too. But love?

He continued down the stairs, his pace slower. A strange heaviness pinched his chest. She hadn't even let him explain, let him tell her his big secret.

And then those stupid flowers and that ring...

If someone was stalking her, then that was cause for alarm.

Fierce protective urges conquered his self-pity, and he charged out into the lobby, intent on doing some digging on Laura's behalf. Though considering how stubborn she was and how pissed she was at him, he doubted she'd take his advice at this point.

With his attention firmly fixed on his phone, he headed for the doors, not really looking where he was going. He collided with someone near the entrance and glanced up to see a guy wearing a dark-colored hoodie similar to his. Distracted, he mumbled an apology and continued out into the bright sunny morning.

Laura might not want his help, but dammit, he refused to give up now.

Not when it meant keeping the woman he loved safe.

18

___

"I need to know everything you've got on Mike McQuade." Laura charged into Blake's office at Rockford Security two hours later. The plaque on his door might've said CEO, but he was still her big brother, and she needed information. "It's urgent."

"Nice to see you too, Sis." Blake swiveled his chair to face her, his expression clearly unfazed by her apparent emergency. "What's up?"

"You sent me to a killer, that's what's up."

"Killer?" He folded his hands calmly on the desk. Growing up with two younger females had made him unflappable. Probably why he was so good at his job. "Explain, please."

"Mike McQuade. You knew he'd been accused of murder, and you didn't say one word to me. Not one damned word." She yanked off her jacket with more force than was necessary and jammed it onto the chair beside her messenger bag. "Then he goes and lies about it and I find out from the cops. The cops, dear brother. Do you know how embarrassing that is? When the cops know more than I do about the guy I'm..." She caught herself before saying more, thankfully. "The guy I'm writing a story about."

Blake blinked at her, his expression stoic. "I assume you're referring to the Lyle Kennedy case, yes?"

Laura crossed her arms and scowled. How could he be so calm about all this? She felt raw, exposed. Betrayed. "Hell yes, I'm talking about Lyle Kennedy."

Blake raised a brow along with his hands. "Language, please. I realize you don't see it as such, but this is a place of business."

"Seriously, Blake? He could've killed me, too."

"Sit down, Laura." Blake came around the desk to lean his hips against it. "Mike's not a killer."

"That's funny," she said, flopping back into her seat. "Because Detective Troy Atkins with the LVPD seems to think he is."

"Then Detective Atkins is mistaken." Blake narrowed his famous glare on her. People hadn't nicknamed it The Hurt for nothing. She shifted in her seat, feeling more like an errant school kid than a grown-ass woman. "I investigated that case myself. It was an accident. What exactly did Troy say?"

"He said that Mike has big secrets he's not telling me."

"And big secrets equal murder, huh?" Blake's expression finally shifted to something other than benign interest. Disappointment. *Ugh.* She wished he would've stayed benign. "I expected more from an accomplished journalist."

"I don't like being lied to."

Blake inhaled deeply and nodded. "Fine. I'll tell you what I know about Mike McQuade if you promise to calm down and stop acting like a two-year-old. And no interruptions."

"Okay. But I—"

He raised an imperious brow at her.

"Fine."

"Fine." He tapped his fingers against the edge of his desk and stared at the floor. "Mike McQuade first hit my radar about eight years ago. There was an altercation involving his younger sister, Reba. Her boyfriend, Lyle Kennedy, was an abuser. His mistreatment landed her in the hospital several times before she finally fought back. We got called out to break up another domestic situation, but before we got there she shot him, killed him. Then she panicked and tried to make it look like an accident. Mike helped her stage it." Blake shrugged. "At first there was suspicion of murder, but we discovered what had really happened soon enough. Wasn't hard. Reba's boyfriend had a rap sheet a mile long. He deserved what he got. The judge ruled it self-defense. Pure and simple. Mike was just trying to protect his little sister. I'd do the same for you in that situation, Laura. You can't hold that against him."

Dammit. Had she been wrong? She hated being wrong about as much as she hated being lied to. A mental picture of Mike, standing in her kitchen earlier looking earnest and sad and entirely too cute for his own good, crossed her frazzled brain. Nope. Not letting him off the hook that easily. "What about the cell phone deal?"

"What cell phone deal?"

"They found a disposable phone at the first crime scene, and Troy said they were trying to trace it back to Mike."

"And that's your proof that Mike McQuade killed two, almost three people?" Blake laughed out loud this time, the sound both astonishing—because of its rarity these days—and thoroughly annoying. "Sis, you know as well as I do those phones are like Kleenex. Millions of people use them every day."

"But I saw a whole stash in the bedroom at his penthouse."

"Okay." Blake straightened slightly. "First off, I'm going to pretend I didn't hear that you've been in his penthouse, since I'm pretty sure I told you specifically not to go there when we started this whole debacle. And second, what the hell were you doing in his bedroom?"

"I..." Heat flooded her cheeks, and she lowered her eyes. "It doesn't matter. I saw them, and there were lots. I'm worried, Blake. What if Mike had something to do with these game-related killings?"

After several silent seconds, Blake cursed under his breath. "Look, I don't know about what the police are investigating or anything about this phone being connected, but I can tell you that Mike couldn't have committed the widow's murder."

"How do you know?"

He gestured for her to follow him behind his desk. Blake took a seat and fired up his computer, clicking several keys until the now familiar security feeds from Turnberry appeared on his screen, showing Mike at the elevator in the lobby. It was time and date stamped for ten p.m. on the night of Barbara Newton's murder. The next video showed him entering his penthouse a few moments later. The third clip didn't show him emerging again until five the next morning.

Blake hit Pause and turned to face her. "The M.E. pinpointed time of death for Barbara Newton at around three a.m."

A smidge of doubt still lingered in Laura's heart. "What about the cameras? Maybe someone messed with the time. Mike's a guru when it comes to all things tech. Troy said it's happened before with the cameras at the El Cortez."

"The El Cortez isn't a Rockford property." He looked

slightly offended by her suggestion. "Nobody messes with my cameras. Nobody."

Well, damn.

Laura walked back around the desk and collapsed into her seat, her face in her hands. What a jerk she'd been earlier. Mike had come all the way over to make sure she was okay, even after she'd reamed him a new one the night before, and she'd done nothing but act like an idiot.

"You didn't really think I'd let my little sister get anywhere near a killer, did you?" Blake asked, his gaze far too perceptive for her taste.

She rubbed her eyes then dropped her hands into her lap. "I don't know what to think anymore. There was something else, too. This morning. Someone sent me red roses and a fake engagement ring. At first I thought they were from Mike, but he denied it when I confronted him."

"I think this Vintage Vegas Killer case is getting to you, that's what I think. Those items could've come from anyone. What about that kid you interviewed a few days ago? The one with the asteroids. You said yourself he was pretty enamored with you, right?"

Yeah, she had said that. That kid practically had stars in his eyes and wedding bells playing in the background when she'd left. Never mind the fact she was twelve years his senior. Maybe Blake was right, anybody could have sent those flowers and that ring. Didn't have to be the killer or anything even related to that damned murder case. And the cheesy ring did seem like something a kid would send.

Her thoughts drifted to Troy. Troy had been outside her apartment last night, and he'd made it clear he wanted more than a professional relationship. Plus the way he'd been insisting she stay away from Mike ...

No, that was crazy. Troy wouldn't send flowers and a ring like that. Would he?

"I can check it out, though, if you want," Blake was saying.

"No." She felt stupid now. "I can clean up my own messes."

"Okay." Blake gave her a once-over, and she did her best not to fidget. "But you're obviously stressed out. I think that once this thing is over and Mike's in the clear, you and he should take a vacation together. Get away from all this and spend some time together."

"Excuse me?"

"You heard me." He smiled, all big-brother confidence. "I got to know Mike McQuade pretty well during that investigation years ago. I think the two of you would make a good couple. Why else do you think I sent you there?"

"Seriously? Who died and made you matchmaker?" She cringed, regretting the words almost immediately. Her brother's wife, his partner on the force and the love of his life, that's who. God, she really was verbally incontinent these days. "I'm sorry. I didn't mean…"

"I know." Pain flickered across his intense, icy-blue eyes before he hid it behind his usual wall of stoicism. "But still, you shouldn't throw away something good with Mike over a misunderstanding. Trust me, life is far too short."

"Right." She took a deep breath then stood. "I think I owe someone an apology."

"Really?" He pulled out a pen and scribbled something on the calendar on his desk.

"What are you doing?"

"Marking this momentous occasion. Laura Rockford admits she's wrong."

She rolled her eyes at him as she left. "Very funny, but thanks for the info."

Laura headed back out to the parking lot. Her stomach rumbled, but she ignored it. She'd be stuffed full of humble pie and crow soon enough. She pulled out and headed back to her apartment, feeling for the first time since she'd started this whole investigation that maybe, just maybe, things might turn out all right after all.

She pulled into a spot half a block from her building and climbed out, texting Mike as she walked toward her entrance. Hopefully he was working from home again today, and hopefully he would answer her message.

At the stoop, she turned, the nape of her neck prickling again.

Someone was still watching her, but there wasn't anyone suspicious around. Only tourists and joggers and a couple walking a cute little dog in a pink sweater. Nope. Blake was right. She had let this crazy case get to her. Definitely time for some R and R after this whole thing was over, if Mike would forgive her and take her back and...

She went to press Send on her phone, but a hand now clamped across her mouth stopped her.

Laura tried to scream, tried to fight back, but her attacker was too strong, and whatever drug soaked the cloth pressed to her face smelled awful and her head felt fuzzy and her vision had gone funny and the last thing she remembered before darkness descended was the overwhelming urge to see Mike once more and tell him how truly sorry she was.

MIKE TYPED another search into his browser, looking for anything that might connect those flowers, that ring to the murders. He had a bad feeling, had even tried going back to Laura's apartment a short time ago, but she'd been gone. So he'd come home to continue his research. She might not want him around, but he'd do everything in his power to protect her.

He pulled up the information on each of the victims again, connecting them all back to the party where Jim had died. The only people he'd invited that night were industry professionals and people from his own company. A quick review of the guest list showed no one living in the immediate vicinity of the crimes or even in Vegas proper.

Which left his own employees.

An unexpected stab of pain sliced through him. He considered his staff part of his family. The possibility that one of their own would do something like this seemed almost impossible. Still, he owed it to Laura to investigate all avenues.

What he wouldn't give to have her here beside him. She'd know what to do with all this information, all these clues. She'd hit it big one day, the national news or whatever she wanted. He was sure of it. Her instincts and her skills were that good. He just hoped he'd be around to see it, to celebrate the accomplishment with her.

He tried calling her phone again, but there was no answer. Went straight to voicemail.

He didn't leave a message.

Instead, Mike focused on the computer screen. No. The best way to help Laura and get back in her good graces was to prove his innocence. So Barbara Newton and Ben Sanders, both dead. Steven Price, attacked but alive. No ties among any of them, except his company.

Why them?

He tried searching through the police reports and the news stories for fresh leads but found none. *Dammit.* He rubbed an exasperated hand over his face and sighed, slumping back in his seat. Picked up his phone again. The tracer was still on Laura's phone. He could just take a peek, see where she was, make sure she was okay.

He tossed the phone aside. That would make him just as bad as the weirdo who'd sent her those flowers this morning. He wanted to be her friend, more if she'd let him. To prove his point, he grabbed the phone again and pressed down on the tracker app then held, waiting for it to quiver. He'd erase the whole program from his phone and be done with it. No more secrets between them.

His finger found the delete button.

Ding.

Mike frowned down at the incoming message. It was from Laura's number but full of odd 1940s jargon:

NO COPPERS SEE?

UPLOAD THE FILE TO THE VEGAS NOIR HOME-PAGE OR THE DAME GETS THE BIG SLEEP.

BEFORE HE COULD REACT to the first message, a second one came in. A photo. Laura, dressed in a vintage wedding gown, her hair in Victory rolls and her makeup done pin-up girl style. From what he could see, she'd been tied to a chair and a gun pointed at her temple.

Fuck.

Frantic, Mike pushed to his feet. He needed to find her, he had to save her.

But first he had to figure out where in the hell she was.

19

———

Laura blinked open heavy-lidded eyes. Everything hurt, her head throbbed, and her mouth ached with dryness. She tried to moan and failed, squinted at the blurriness surrounding her then focused on her lap. White. White fabric everywhere. As far as she could remember, she'd worn jeans that day. Jeans and a navy-blue sweater, not white...

She attempted to reach for the fabric but found her hands secured behind her back. Tried to move her legs, too. Nope. Tied as well.

Shit.

Despite her pounding head, she did her best to concentrate. She'd been at her building, ready to text Mike, then...

Oh God.

Her attacker must've drugged her, that was it. The

acrid stench of whatever substance he'd used still lingered in her nose and throat, making her stomach riot. She dry-swallowed and took a deep breath to steady her racing pulse. Calm. She had to stay calm. That's what Liv had taught her. Assailants counted on their victims getting stupid with fear, doing irrational things to escape. By staying calm, she could keep the upper hand, buy herself some precious time, stay in control.

A voice filtered into her hazy reality, male and tense and vaguely familiar.

"Dammit. Why doesn't he upload the file?"

She raised her head slightly, hoping to still appear unconscious while she scoped out her location, her enemy. From the stained glass and altar before her, it appeared she was being held in some kind of chapel or church. Rows of long pews stretched out before her, a lone man sitting in the front one, dressed in a black hoodie.

As if sensing her gaze, he turned fast and caught her staring. "Oh, you're awake. Good. Guess your boyfriend doesn't care enough to save you."

Ted? Mike's twitchy right-hand man?

She exhaled and stared at her lap again, noticed the beading and intricate stitch work. A wedding dress? In a wedding chapel? At least the fake engagement ring made sense now. The Wedding at the Little Church of the West was the highest level in *Vegas Noir*. She wasn't good enough at the game to have gotten there yet, but she'd seen it on the fan sites. She shook her head slightly, then winced as her world went cockeyed again.

Guess I should've seen this one coming.

Laura gripped the ropes around her wrists tighter and jerked hard, testing their strength. Her movement caused the chair to scrape against the floor, and Ted stood, gun in hand.

"Don't even think about trying to escape. You won't make it."

"Why are you doing this?" Her voice creaked out like an old floorboard. "Mike's your friend, your mentor. Why would you want to destroy him?"

"Right." He gave a derisive snort. "If that's what you think then you're not the brilliant reporter you like to think you are. No wonder they give you nothing but fluff to cover."

A twinge of anger coursed through her regardless of the fact she was tied to a chair with a literal gun to her head. She might be covering fluff, but she wouldn't be forever, dammit. Especially after tonight. "What makes you think you can get away with this? Mike's a genius when it comes to tech."

"No." Ted stepped closer, his dour expression deepening with fury. "He *was* a genius. Not anymore. Especially not now. Not with you around. All he thinks about anymore is you. It's pathetic."

Her heart leapt at his words despite the situation. Mike thought about her all the time? Mike was distracted by her? She was certainly guilty of the same where he was concerned, but he was so secretive and hard to read, and now she might die and never know if he might care about her as much as she cared about him and...

Fresh adrenaline surged through her bloodstream.

Keep calm. Get a grip. Keep him talking while you figure out a plan...

Liv's voice, her sister's voice, kept ringing through her head, cutting through her hysteria-fueled bullshit and setting her back on course. *Get out, get free, get safe. Then worry about Mike.* Seemed like a great idea, until Ted's next words crash landed her resolve.

"Besides, Mike's already taken the fall. I've been feeding clues to the police. Now all he has to do is upload the file to the homepage of the M Cubed website like I asked and it's done. If not, then I'll have to go with my Plan B."

"Plan B?"

He raised the gun and mock pulled the trigger at her, his wide smile chilling.

Shit. Shit. Shit.

Keep him talking, keep him talking, keep him talking...

"So, uh, what file?"

"The one connecting all the final dots for the cops. Showing Mike at the first crime scene touching the body. Showing Mike going to that café, the one right next door to where the second victim was found. Showing Mike schmoozing with the gal in accounting and linking victim number three to him and his company. I emailed it to him and now all he has to do is upload the file replacing the M Cubed homepage with the incriminating photos. I'd do it myself but he's got that file locked for access. Only he can upload it."

Mike was at the first crime scene?

"What are you talking about? Mike didn't kill Barbara Newton."

"No, but he couldn't resist responding to my text luring him to the crime scene. Couldn't resist bending over the poor widow. The added bonus was that he also couldn't resist playing the good guy. Had to be the hero and call 9-1-1 on that disposable phone. I saw the cops put it in an evidence bag, and with any luck they'll be able to trace it to him. Another nail in his coffin." He shrugged. "Then, of course, I'll add in you. Can't forget his little obsession with his favorite reporter."

"Obsession?"

"Yeah. It's what drove him to kill you, after all. Obsession can be a very motivating factor."

"Where's Mike now?"

"Don't know, don't care. That's the beauty of it. Doesn't matter where he is. I've already done the hard part, pointing all fingers toward him, including staging the first crime scene exactly like the pictures that crazy photographer sent him that the cops will find in his apartment. You were just the icing on the cake. Even if you did almost ruin everything by sticking your nose in where it didn't belong. Then again, all your prying gives it an authenticity that was lacking before, makes Mike look even more unstable. And those flowers. A nice touch, if I do say so myself."

Ted turned away to check his laptop again, and Laura fiddled with the ropes once more. If she could just get a hand free, she could wriggle out and smack him over the head with her chair. In the background, Ted continued to grumble.

"Such a damned control freak. All those dumbass firewalls. Have to have the right security to upload. *No, Ted, you're not good enough. No, Ted, only I can have access.* Freaking moron."

Ted rubbed his nose, revealing a blackish-purple bruise beneath what must've been several layers of makeup. Details from her conversation with Steven Price trickled back into her fevered brain.

He might've screamed like a girl when I punched him, but he was a guy...

Ted hadn't brought Mike's coffee the next day, claiming illness, but he wasn't sick, he was recovering from being punched by Steven Price.

She'd like to punch Ted too, if she could just get out of these damned restraints.

A thump sounded outside the double doors behind her.

Maybe that was the police, maybe she'd get out of

this alive after all. She silently rose up on the balls of her feet to move her chair a bit more to the side, away from the doors in case the cops burst through. She didn't want to get trampled. Laura leaned her head back and discovered the chair had a high, wooden back. If worse came to worst, she might be able to jam it into her captor's already damaged nose, gaining her precious time to kick his weapon away and get out.

Ted set his laptop aside and moved toward her again. Just a couple more steps, one, two, and he'd be close enough she could bop him good with the back of the chair. If she hit him hard enough, maybe she could even force his septum up into his brain, killing him instantly. Liv had told her it was possible, though she'd never had reason to want to try it until now.

C'mon. Just a little bit closer. C'mon...

The door behind her opened, and she and Ted both turned in unison.

"Mike!" Her exclamation echoed in the silent chapel.

Ted aimed the gun at Mike's chest. "Don't come any closer, or I'll end you. I swear I will."

"Ted, please. Put the gun down," Mike said, his hands raised in surrender. "You don't have to do this. There's still a way out."

"Damn straight there is." He pointed the weapon at Laura again. "You want her to live? Then upload that damn file and do exactly as I say. Otherwise I'll blow her brains out."

"What exactly is in that file?" Mike inched closer to Laura with each word, his gaze meeting hers briefly before darting back to Ted.

"The final piece of the puzzle the cops need to convict you. Those idiots could never compile the evidence, so I took the privilege of doing it for them. The widow, the caterer, Jim Newton."

"Jim?" Mike's stoic façade fractured. "That was an accident."

"Accident my ass. That drug I slipped in his drink worked better than I hoped. Made the alcohol that much more potent, and the coroner never even thought to look for it. Now Jim's cremated and the evidence is long gone. Pretty damned genius, if you ask me. Besides, how else was I going to get his job, huh? You wouldn't even give me the time of day back then." Ted chuckled. "Of course, all the money we've made since then has changed your attitude, hasn't it, boss? At least where my work is concerned."

Laura glanced sideways and saw Mike's hands clenched at his sides, his knuckles white with the pressure.

"Too bad about the widow, though," Ted continued, oblivious. "Barbara was nice. If she hadn't stirred things up, she wouldn't have had to die. But then I walked in on your little conversation, and I knew what I had to do."

"You son of a bitch."

"Bailey. Son of a Bailey. My last name's Bailey, but then you never really cared enough to notice, did you?"

"That's what this is all about? Recognition? You were going to get equal billing on the new game, you know that."

"Equal billing?" Ted scoffed. "Full billing, that's what I deserved. I designed that whole thing, built that game from the ground up. All you did was critique and tweak. Then, of course, you took up with this new piece of ass, and then you didn't even do that much."

"Leave Laura out of this." Mike's normally smooth tone turned lethal.

"Well, see. That's the thing, Mike." Ted gave him a small, cold sneer. "I can't do that. Not now. She's digging into things that are none of her business. And honestly, she provides the one thing I couldn't do on my own."

Mike moved closer, close enough for her to feel his heat against the chilled skin of her bare shoulder. She took strength from his warmth, his nearness. His fingers brushed her flesh, and she shuddered. He glanced down at her fast, concern and warning in his brown eyes, before he looked away. "What's that, Ted?"

"Getting you to confess. Once you upload the file, it'll be on the main page of the *Vegas Noir* website for the world to see. Crazy recluse like you, who wouldn't believe it, huh? You got too involved in your own game, started acting it out in real life, then Laura came along, and she grew into your new obsession. But she rejected you. You couldn't take that, the rejection. It was an insult to your geeky genius. So you killed her, then out of guilt and desperation you turned the gun on yourself. Murder-suicide. Kind of a poetic justice in that, don't you think?"

Ted reached over and grabbed his laptop with his free hand. "Now, I'll just need to make one small edit to the file, and it will all fall seamlessly into place."

As he concentrated on his computer, Mike nudged Laura's shoulder once more, raising a brow in Ted's direction, giving her a now-or-never look. *Right.* She braced her legs against the floor once more and gripped the ropes around her wrists tight then leaned forward and rammed the chair forward with all her might.

Facing the floor as she was, she could only see the feet of the two men as they struggled, but judging from Ted's high-pitched wails, she'd struck her mark. Steven Price had been right. Ted did scream like a girl.

The impact had shattered the back of her chair enough that she was able to wiggle her hands from the ropes then set about untying her ankles.

Before she was free, however, a gunshot fired.

Laura screamed and Ted wailed then dropped to his knees, blood gushing from his leg now as well as his nose. *Serves him right, the bastard.*

Sirens wailed outside and cops burst in, led by Troy and followed by Blake.

Troy gave her a quick once-over then headed over to help place Ted under arrest.

"I don't need help." She snapped at Blake, who had rushed to her side. She was annoyed with her still-drugged, fumbling fingers at not being able to undo the knots around her feet. Realizing Blake was just trying to help, voice softened. "I've got this under control."

"Yeah, Sis. I can see that." Blake leaned down and placed an affectionate kiss on the top of her head. "I'm glad you're okay. I heard the call come in over the scanner, and after I'd checked out those flowers you mentioned earlier, I figured I better assess the situation myself to be sure."

"Checked out? What are you talking about? I told you not to worry about those flowers."

"Hey, big brother prerogative, okay?" Blake held up his hands and winked. "Like I said, I'd never let my little sister get anywhere near a killer."

He kissed her hair once more then tilted his head toward Mike, who'd now rushed over to undo her ankles. "You take good care of her, understand?"

Mike glanced up at Blake, and some weird, silent guy-communication occurred between them that Laura didn't quite grasp. Blake nodded and left, leaving her alone with Mike, his hands on her legs, chaffing her abraded skin.

"Are you all right, Princess?" He leaned closer, the

corners of his warm brown eyes crinkled with concern. "If he hurt you at all, I swear to God I will—"

"I'm fine." She placed her fingers over his mouth, forgetting about the cops and Ted's girly whining. Forgetting about everything except Mike kneeling before her. "Are you okay?"

"I am now." He leaned closer, brushing his lips over hers, once, twice, before capturing her mouth with his. When they finally broke apart, they were both breathless. Mike leaned his forehead against hers and took her trembling hands in his, lacing their fingers together.

"Hey, I hate to break up this touching moment," Troy said, walking past them with a defeated, howling Ted in tow. "But I need to question you both."

"Later, Troy," Laura said, her attention still firmly on the man whose head still leaned against hers.

"Regulations state that—"

"*Later*, Troy." Laura turned her head slightly to glare at him. "Tomorrow, okay? You owe me for this big bust anyway."

Troy shook his head and exhaled. "Fine. Tomorrow, Rockford. But this makes us even, okay? No more favors."

She smiled. "No more favors. Thanks, Troy."

Troy hauled Ted out the door then gave her a small smile in return. "You're welcome, Rockford. Tomorrow, ten a.m. Don't be late."

"We won't." She turned back to Mike and cupped his cheek. "How'd you know I was here, anyway?"

Mike shrugged, a hint of amusement and heat creeping into his gaze. "Let's just say I have my ways."

"Ways, huh? Wouldn't have anything to do with a certain tracking app I found on my phone, would it?"

"You knew about that?" For the first time since she'd met him, genius Mike McQuade looked genuinely stunned. "How?"

Laura chuckled and threw his words right back at him. "Let's just say I have my ways."

"Hmm." He pulled her off the chair and into his arms. "No more secrets between us from now on, yes?"

"Yes." Laura threaded her fingers through his hair, just the way she knew he loved. "No more secrets ever."

20

―――――

"You're not nervous, are you?" Laura asked from beside Mike, squeezing his hand tight in hers as the car he'd hired pulled up in front of Blake Rockford's Summerlin home. "You don't have to be. They'll love you."

"Maybe a little, I guess." He met her eyes then lowered his gaze. "This is a bit out of my comfort zone. I'm not exactly a social butterfly like you guys."

"Hey." She tipped his chin up with her fingers. "My family will love you. You're the smartest, kindest, most generous man I've ever known. And I'll be by your side the whole time, okay?"

"Okay." He got out then held out his hand to help her. Mike then leaned back inside and told the driver he'd call when they were ready to leave. After shutting the door, he thumped on the roof as the town car pulled away. Straightening his shirt and smoothing his damp palms down his jeans-covered thighs for the umpteenth time, he sighed. "Let's do this."

"Smile. It's not a firing squad."

"Why does it feel like that, then?" He forced what he hoped was a polite grin as they approached the door.

Laura rang the bell then glanced at him, snickering. "You look like you're petrified."

"I *am* petrified."

Shouts rang through the door before it was yanked open. Blake grinned then waved them inside. "Welcome to the asylum."

Inside, people young and old milled about, talking and laughing and playing games, all of them related in one way or another to Laura. Mike's family was much smaller, spread around the country now, and his sister Reba was the only sibling he had any regular contact with. After today, he had a feeling his life and his family had just gotten a little more crowded.

"Can I get you something to drink, Mike?" Blake asked, clapping him on the shoulder.

"Uh, water, please."

"Sure." Blake gestured toward the room. "Make yourself comfortable. Obviously everyone else does. Sis, you want something?"

"White wine, please?"

"Got ya."

"Well, if it isn't the star reporter herself." A tall guy,

slightly older than Laura but with the same dark hair and hazel eyes, approached. In his hands was that morning's *Chronicle*, featuring Laura's byline and a huge headline—Vintage Vegas Killer Arraigned. Court Date Set. "Congrats, Sis."

He leaned in to kiss Laura on the cheek and she reciprocated.

"Thanks. Logan, this is Mike McQuade. Mike, this is my older brother, Logan Rockford."

"You design those video games, huh?" Logan asked, a beer bottle clutched in one hand.

"Yeah."

"Maybe you can help me out with something later. My buddies and I have been stuck on level twenty-eight of *Witch Wars* for weeks, and we can't figure it out."

"That's not one of mine, sorry." Mike grinned. "I can probably give you some pointers, though."

"Awesome." Logan backed away and gave Mike a call-me gesture then winked at Laura.

"Here you guys go," Blake said, returning with their drinks. "So, things settling down at the company again?"

"Yeah," Mike cracked open the lid on his water bottle. "I still need to find a replacement for Ted, but otherwise things are good. I'm thinking of going more for a group effort than a single person for second in command."

"That concept has worked for me," Blake said, taking a swig of his soda. "If I think of anyone who might be a good fit for your team, I'll send 'em your way."

"Thanks."

Another woman came up, stunningly beautiful and crisp looking, though slightly out of place in her business suit among all the jeans and sweatshirts. "Hey, sis." She kissed Laura as well, then extended a hand to Mike. "Olivia Rockford. You can call me Liv. Everyone else does. And I *knew* you guys were perfect for each other."

Laura elbowed her hard in the side. "Liv, shut up. You didn't know any such thing."

"Hey, it's a gift. What can I say?" She grinned at Mike and leaned closer. "Welcome to the family."

"Uh, thanks." Heat prickled up his neck from beneath this shirt collar. Welcome to the *family*? That sounded serious and permanent. Not that Mike minded. It had only been two weeks since the murders had been solved and only a month since he'd met Laura for the first time. But he already knew she was the one, and something told him he'd have to be on his toes around her siblings. "Glad to be here."

"Okay, guys." Blake whistled loud to quiet the horde. "Dinner is served."

"I'll introduce you to my parents once we're seated."

"Okay." He tugged her aside as the rest of her family filed into the dining room. "Hey, thanks for inviting me, Princess."

"I wouldn't want to attend a family dinner with anyone else." She kissed him sweetly then pulled him toward the door. "Ready for the future?"

Mike smiled, his chest bursting with joy and hope for the first time in years. Laura had brought about that miraculous change, taking his life from bleak loneliness to pure happiness. And now that he'd found it, found her, he planned to show her just how much he treasured her gift. Every day, for the rest of his life, if she'd let him. "More than you'll ever know, Princess. More than you'll ever know."

****

Book 3 in the Rockford Series is available now! If you like a story with lots of twists, then you'll love No One To Trust where a brutal murder pits an innocent man against a killer in a manipulative game of cat and mouse:

NO ONE TO TRUST

JOIN my readers list to get new release notifications:
http://ladobbs.com/newsletter

DID you know that I write mysteries under other names? Join the LDobbs reader group on Facebook and find out! It's a fun group where I give out inside scoops on my books and we talk about reading!
https://www.facebook.com/groups/ldobbsreaders

ALSO BY L. A. DOBBS

Sam Mason Mysteries

***

Telling Lies (Book 1)

Keeping Secrets (Book 2)

Exposing Truths (Book 3)

Betraying Trust (Book 4)

Killing Dreams (Book 5)

More books in the Rockford Security Series:

Cold As Her Heart

A Game of Kill

No One To Trust

No Time To Run

Don't Fear The Truth

Hide From The Past

ABOUT THE AUTHOR

L. A. Dobbs also writes light mysteries as USA Today Bestselling author Leighann Dobbs. Lee has had a passion for reading since she was old enough to hold a book, but she didn't put pen to paper until much later in life. After a twenty-year career as a software engineer, she realized you can't make a living reading books, so she tried her hand at writing them and discovered she had a passion for that, too! She lives in New Hampshire with her husband, Bruce, their trusty Chihuahua mix, Mojo, and beautiful rescue cat, Kitty.

Her book "Dead Wrong" won the "Best Mystery Romance" award at the 2014 Indie Romance Convention.

Her book "Ghostly Paws" was the 2015 Chanticleer Mystery & Mayhem First Place category winner in the Animal Mystery category.

Join her VIP Readers group on Facebook:
https://www.facebook.com/groups/ldobbsreaders

Find out about her L. A. Dobbs Mysteries at:
http://www.ladobbs.com

This is a work of fiction.

None of it is real. All names, places, and events are products of the author's imagination. Any resemblance to real names, places, or events are purely coincidental, and should not be construed as being real.

Fatal Games

Copyright © 2016-2019

L. A. Dobbs

All Rights Reserved.

No part of this work may be used or reproduced in any manner, except as allowable under "fair use," without the express written permission of the author.

✽ Created with Vellum